For All $He's Worth

A Novel by

Max Deveraux

ISBN: 978-0-9992842-9-2

For All $He Worth
Soft-cover edition 2018

For more information about special discounts for bulk purchases, please contact us at: bpcpublishing@gmail.com

Bellucci, Palms & Carmichael Publishing, LLC

Dedication

To all those unfortunate ones who fell victim to mistaken entity and could no longer recognize their former soulmates, but met their new cellmates in the Super-Max prison of failed love...called Family Court

Acknowledgments

I would like to thank all those wonderful people who encouraged me along the way. My family and my professors at UCLA. A very special "thank you" to Candice De Long who unbeknownst to her, helped me get an understanding and affinity to appreciate the remarkable work of FBI Criminal Profilers.

Prologue

This is a work of fiction. It is not autobiographical nor are the situations described herein about the life of any real person. Any similarities to specific people or situations are unintentional, and proves the point that it could happen to any of us.

I, Arlie Everstone, was inspired to write it because of a phenomenon I had – the displeasure of witnessing.

A friend of mine, poor thing, she's going through a tough divorce.

She's tall, about 5'7", long legs, blonde, sexy, smart, accomplished. And she's sweet as hell. The type one loves to secretly hate for no reason; perhaps because she's always had it all.

But she's not the typical Beverly Hills house-wife.

She and some of our college sorority sisters were having dinner at a swank (really overpriced) Hollywood haunt. At the end of the meal, while several of the girls were engaged in an animated exchange using their cell phones to calculate and itemize each other's share of the bill and tip, she broke the sad news to us that her marriage was over.

At first, we all feigned hurt and care. Then one of our sorors gave her, the tried and true advice we have used with our other friends in similar situations.

"Ok girl this is war, so you better pull yourself together by your thong and man-up, then take his sorry ass for all he's worth."

My friend responded, "I would if I could, but it's not that type of party."

"What do you mean?" Asked the advice giver.

"He hasn't made any money for years, and it's more likely: For all I'm worth."

With our mouths agape, in unison we collectively sighed, "Dang Girl!"

We dropped our heads and looked down.

~

Until then I had never heard of women paying men alimony or spousal support. I thought it was a laughable joke until several of my female coworkers and business associates told me the horror stories they were experiencing and it got me pondering about how common this reversal had become.

I started doing some investigating on my own on all this:

In a 2012 survey published in the Huffington Post and the Daily Mail by the Matrimonial Lawyers Association, 56% of the lawyers reporting had experienced increases in woman payers of child support, and 47% saw increases in alimony over the prior three years. Women were out-enrolling men in college 65% to 35% and advancing in the workplace, this trend suggests potentially it could become a societal norm.

As women have broken through the glass ceiling to bridge the gap toward equality, they have been greeted with a "Toll Fee" as it were, as the opportunity-cost for their hard work and success. One can recall the high profile divorce settlements of former Yahoo CEO Susan Decker; actress Anne Heche; performer Britney Spears, singer and actress Mary J. Blige; and countless other lesser knowns.

Some piercing questions arise:

Perhaps one can agree that equality does demand that we all pay our fair share, but does one also believe that able-bodied people should prey on others to pay their way? Does a lifestyle maintenance guarantee come as a birthright? If not, why should one come with a separation or divorce? Does this pseudo private welfare system just like its public counterpart, discourage personal responsibility and preparation? Should the old adage of "Marrying Well" be replace by the New Age strategy of "Divorcing Well?" Should the default "Plan B" be…To Take Her/Him For All They're Worth?

Ever since then I've been listening to a number of friends and acquaintances bemoan their frustration about their relationship situations and how they were about to pursue the "Nuclear Option" of getting a divorce, I was dumbfounded by how ignorant we all are when it comes to how the legalities of separation play out.

This ignorance is costly and sometimes deadly.

Many are unaware that when they signed the marriage license they were actually signing a prenuptial agreement negotiated by the state without their input. They have never been given a copy of it nor an acknowledgement that they have had the opportunity to read the fine print.

This violates the principal of Full Disclosure. This would be illegal in any contractual situation and enforceable by state law but that same state violates its own laws routinely and with impunity.

While most view marriage as the consecration of a religious rite of passage or the ultimate expression of love and commitment, that's not how the state views it; remember the state is by constitution religiously and, by definition, love neutral. As harsh as it may sound, to the state (not me) it's a mere commercial business contract. No matter what one thinks, what one feels is fair, or one's religious affiliation: its state rules, and The State Rules! To that I say: Caveat Emptor!

When the reality of this mega shock to the system sets in, it normally leads to predictable feelings of anger, self-loathing, and disillusionment. However increasingly in some cases it has led to homicidal murder.

Ask any family lawyer and they will confirm that by design, marriage is cheap and easy to get into but expensive and extremely difficult to get out of. Where is the consistency? Selective history tells us that strong family bonds make for a healthy society but should those bonds when broken become a debt instrument?

Case in point, and this is a true story. Once a fiancé (BTW - By-The-Way - I often marvel that fiancé and finance had similar spelling just separated ironically by an "n"), complain to me that my own desire to have a prenuptial agreement, in her opinion "took the love out of the relationship," I responded "nope it takes the money out of the relationship and what's left is the love."

Well needless to say: I'm still single.

For the record I am personally a strong proponent of marriage. However, I'm also an even stronger opponent of ignorance whether it is through deception, oversight or by decree. Ask any friend of mine and they will tell you I have an affinity to watch some bad TV of the Real Crime ilk. Although I deplore murder (no matter how rational it may seem), the science of finding out the "who donnit" is addicting.

The sad truth is more and more of my female friends have been getting the proverbial shaft in divorce cases. More and more successful women now have to pay guys to go away?

To me that's way out of whack!

Should one decide to enter the ring of love or just wear the ring, one should have fun and enjoy but should also be prepared to bob and weave if one dares to climb out.

This makes one think twice; about getting married, three times about divorce and at least once about murder.

~

One afternoon I got a call from Agent Nolen that there was something major going down at the courthouse.

"Arlie, get here now!"

I must have broken all traffic rules, I sped away to the action as if I had accoutrements of lights and sirens!

By the time I got there it was pure pandemonium, total chaos.

From the very start it felt as if this would be my lucky break of a lifetime. It did turn out to be the biggest story that I could have ever imagined!

~

Knowing for a few months in advance that the Internet was about to claim the life of another local paper (that being my employer); I had an epiphany: 'I only live a few miles from Hollywood, so why don't I pitch my own Real Crime Reality TV Show!'

Brilliant I thought!

The problem is however, proximity does not equal familiarity and I really didn't know anybody in Hollywood. That was one problem. The other was I needed a story to pitch.

That's when it hit me…

It changed my career from lowly beat reporter to television producer and narrator…!

At least the name of the show hit me!

"For All $He's Worth."

1

I'm addicted.

No, actually I'm obsessed. There, I've finally admitted it.

Now I feel better owning up to my insatiable desire to watch true crime shows. I'm not alone, it's the fastest growing genre on TV.

I don't like crime or blood or gore. I'm more interested in why people do the crimes that they do but most of all, I like how crimes are solved. I especially love the saucy stories about love gone wrong. Oh, and I love forensics, too!

One of the things that intrigues me the most is when a seemingly normal person snaps or goes berserk and does some astonishingly heinous murder and thinks she or he can get away with it!

One takes the biggest risk of his or her life doing something, which they have the lowest skill set in doing and then are surprised when they get caught?

It's laughable as it is brazen!

It shows that anybody and I mean *everybody* is capable of murder if the right motivation, opportunity and means are present at the same time! This is especially true when it involves someone you love. Because, love and hate are the mirror extremes of the same emotion.

As much as I love crime solving, I'm also afraid of guns, but becoming a detective was out of the question. Even though I admire scientists I can't see myself in a white lab coat and as far as talking to some other geeks about esoteric subjects, no, no, no! So no lab work for me.

I am a people's person. That is why I chose journalism.

The power of the pen is at times more powerful than the sword.

I'm still currently working the crime beat at the soon to be defunct neighborhood newspaper. It doesn't pay much (and sometimes not at all) but it does have its perks. I get insider leads on crime stories, I go on "ride-a-longs" with patrol officers, and my donut shop reviews on Yelp have become legendary!

Ride-a-long's are okay, but after a while one gets tired of the same old domestic stuff: "Twisted-Faced" drunken ex-boyfriends not wanting it to be over, making a total fool of themselves by yelling and banging on doors and scaring the crap out of the neighbors and then getting bitten on their butts by dogs. Then the occasional dumped "Psycho" ex-girlfriend doing a straight Jackson Pollack on some poor guy's car with battery acid.

I'm not saying this isn't serious crime, because god knows it can escalate to real violence.

But I like action!

This might sound kinda' insensitive but for some reason it does not bothered me in the least.

I don't know, maybe it's my Asperger-thing syndrome.

Go figure!

~

In all my years of investigative journalism I have come across murders both brilliant and stupid. The one common denominator that links them, is the irreversible infliction of death. Entry in this club, levels the playing field, where fools and geniuses compete to commit the perfect crime. The winner is forever enshrined with hands stained in crimson blood and the loser is bound by rust in handcuffs.

I have observed that murder is not a profession exclusive to kings and nobles. There is no graduate school or even a certificate program you must pass to qualify. You only need to obey your MOM! Yes all you need is Motive, Opportunity and Means. This low barrier to entry extends a perverse invitation to us all without prejudice as to one's pedigree, education or station in life. Murder is the ultimate model of egalitarianism.

Admittedly, murder is a sport in which one can almost find oneself on the sidelines rooting for someone to perfectly commit.

Perhaps it gives the spectator amongst us – hope. Yet not for the lack of ingenuity on the part of the participant, the fact remains: the perfect crime is just the crime that has yet to be committed. It's an illusion for some and a preoccupation for others. Detection may be deferred, but perfection seems to have a shelf life that's getting shorter.

As clever as the criminal mind has evolved so have the tools to snare it. These opposing forces are locked in a death spiral as if they were challenging each other to sharpen its edge. It is remarkable how elaborate some of the schemes are. The detail. The sophistications. The expense. The folly.

No matter what the motive or rationale, be it righteous or senseless, it is not in the best interest of the executioner to get caught and they will do everything within the power of their imagination to avoid this. It's then left up to the police to reverse engineer the construction of the elusive perfect murder and find its structural weakness.

I will take you into the lab, the bastions of higher learning, into the dark corners of cyberspace and unto halls of justices.

We will observe the struggle of our better angels with our base impulses as they contend for dominance.

Warning: It may test the limits of one's suppressed criminal imagination and stretch one's definition of fair play.

~

As uncovered and unbeknownst at the time to the newly minted divorcee Dr. Sumi Kim, a Geneticist and Bio-Technologist, it all started while she was being stalked. Stalked, not by a predator, but by a fellow scientist. Not as his prey but as his potential test subject.

At her final divorce settlement hearing in the Family Law section of the Superior Courts building in downtown Los Angeles, Sumi's case was being observed by Niles, a Professor of Evolutionary Psychology and research scientist.

Along with his doctoral candidate Tiffany Lane, Niles was in the midst of doing groundbreaking work on the causal relationship between divorce and spousalcide.

Sumi was looking for relief and Niles was looking for laboratory mice of the human variety.

Feeling damaged by the failure of her marriage, the last thing in the world, the shy and reserved Sumi wished for, was to bring attention to herself but that wish was not going to be granted. The young and brilliant scientist not only found herself with her personal intimate secrets on public display but in an ironic twist she unwittingly became a key player in helping solve one of the most creative murders of our time.

Sumi was mindful of the fact that her innovative scientific discoveries had game-changing potential for law enforcement. What she didn't anticipate however was her personal and professional circumstances were on a collision course and that she would be thrust into a situation that had both her and her inventions play a direct role in the identification and apprehension of a skillful but demented murderer.

~

I will reveal the intricacies and explore the labyrinth of academia, technology, moral failure and justice.

By the end of this journey one will think twice about marriage, three times about divorce and at least once about murder.

2

"All rise, the honorable judge Roland Pierce presiding," bellowed the deep-throated and portly female bailiff.

Judge Pierce enjoyed a reputation for being equally fair-minded and would always play by the book, while maintaining an empathetic disposition to all parties – a trifecta not common amongst his peers. Ironically, Roland Pierce never wanted to be a family law judge. Earlier on in his career he was on the fast track to becoming head-justice in criminal law division, specializing in white-collar crime. If not for a literal twist of fate causing him to be late for a third time to a twice-postponed hearing and an unsympathetic judge punishing him by assigning him to a pro-bono and gut-wrenching child custody case, he arguably could have made it in the big-time and even bigger rewards of high-powered corporate litigation. That one unexpected but life-altering case put a reluctant Roland Pierce on a new life's mission: first, as the voice of helpless children whose highest and best use was as a hammer and anvil, and at worst, a bargaining chip during divorce disputes; and second, the booty of family warfare.

"I have carefully reviewed the merits of this case, taking in consideration the requests of all parties and the circumstances, which bring us to this point. However, before I rule, experience has shown me that it is helpful to all to be reminded of the limitations of the law.

"The law is not designed to resolve all the issues laid before the court. Oh no, quite the contrary, for many of these issues can only be resolved by time and the help of professionals such as psychologists, counselors, and pastors. Justice makes no grandiose claims of being a divine healer of the wounded. I am a judge, I am no Solomon.

"But what we do have here is a set of legal, albeit narrow guidelines developed over many years and codified by precedence of case law, with the goal of neutralizing the burdens on all parties: plaintiff, defendant, and the state. Unfortunately, this lofty goal is seldom reached.

"Therefore, whether you agree with my decisions or not, you must understand that this is the system that we as a collective society have agreed upon in these types of disputes. Having said that, do any of the parties wish to address the court before my ruling is handed down?"

Dwayne Stephens, tried to control his impulse to leap up and remind the judge that he didn't want a divorce, and that his wife of ten years refused all treatments for her severe addiction to methamphetamines, better known by its street moniker, "crystal-meth." She initiated divorce proceedings as an ingenious way to obtain a steady flow of funds to maintain her, and her fellow 'tweeker' boyfriend's habit.

As the tension in his stomach rose to audible levels, Dwayne's lawyer's hand clamped around his forearm. Her oft-repeated assurances that 'things will work out just fine' reverberating in his head, kept him pinned to his seat.

The two replies of "No your honor," repeated in close succession by both counsels as if in an echo chamber, would be remembered by Dwayne like the loop of a scratched record replaying his last rites.

In his characteristically modulated and even-toned dispassionate voice, Judge Pierce read from his notes, "In respects to the plaintiff's petition for spousal support, the court accepts the results from the Disso-Master computer program and awards her 40% of the household gross income and 50% of all community property."

A suffused cry struggled to burst through the restriction of Dwayne's frozen vocal cords like the panicked wheezing of a person gasping for oxygen, attempting to wrestle his life back from the vice-grip of death brought about by severe sleep apnea.

The only intelligible words Dwayne could manage were, "But, but it's not fair…ugh…it's not fair."

The alarmed Judge Pierce looked up from the papers he was reading and asked, "Is there something wrong?"

Dwayne shouted, "It's just not fair! I didn't ask for this divorce. It's, it's just not fair that I have to pay so she can abuse drugs!"

Judge Pierce calmly said, "I know son but I have no choice. This is how the system works."

As Dwayne continued his protest, the judge strongly admonished his lawyer to restrain his client.

'Poor S.O.B.' thought Niles, as he sat taking the whole drama in from the back of the courtroom.

~

Niles, who had spent a good sum of his time as a spectator of the blood sport of XX versus XY, had seen it all before. To him this was a pathetic, albeit typical outcome of the daily battles in California's family law courts: higher wage earning spouses paying the freight for lower earning and often undeserving spouses. He thought, 'Judges have become impotent – their discretion ruled by the cold calculations of the Almighty Disso-Master' – the computerized divorce asset and income divider.

Although the current state of affairs of the judicial system bothered Niles Racine, his 26 years as an Evolutionary Psychology professor at UCLA had prepared him to stay objective.

To Niles, this was all about research. He was fascinated if not obsessed with the question of what motivated humans to behave the way they did. Early in his career, he developed a specialization in family law forensics with emphasis in psychopathic behavior.

Niles welcomed this current assignment, as it allowed him to get out of the lab and do real world field research.

To assist him, was his current Doctoral Candidate Tiffany Lane; Niles had agreed to visit the courts and select subjects for the third part-online therapy of her doctoral research project.

'Yes,' thought Niles, 'just another sap being fleeced by a system – its original intent having long been lost. The pendulum has swung wildly out of control.'

Sadly as it was, this case was one of thousands. 'On to the next courtroom.'

Niles left Dwayne Stephens in his misery.

~

As he lingered in the hallway of the court house, Niles overheard two lawyers in a hushed exchange.

"Look, give me a little help here and I'll see what I can do about the supervision issue on Lauder-back's, okay?"

"Not so fast big guy, I was hoping to stretch this one out a little longer. I need the hours this month."

"As long as we agree in principal, I'll keep my client dancing. But you're gonna owe me one."

Before walking into courtroom 211, Niles thought, 'Not justice but backroom deals keep the legal profession thriving. No wonder the only winners in this area of law are the lawyers themselves as they walk over the bones of broken people hunting for their next kill.'

Niles mused as he looked over the court docket, 'Hmm, this ought to be interesting.' He'd heard about these types of cases but rarely got a chance to witness the tables being turned. In this case, a philandering ex-husband was suing a professional woman for alimony.

'It's only going to get worse with women now out-enrolling men 6 to 4 in higher education,' he thought. 'The coming gap in income and intellect might well level the playing field.'

The husband in this case was very good in the sack but as it turned out that's all he was good for. He was much better at being bad.

Niles was expecting to see a lot less than what was unfolding before his eyes. Expecting an over-fit, hard-charging, card-carrying corporate Fem-Nazi, he was surprised to see a forty-something non-descript and soft-spoken woman.

One could see Sumi Kim-Phelps a hundred times in a hundred days and swear one had never laid eyes on her.

This intrigued Niles all the more.

The plaintiff instead was extraordinarily handsome… tall, blond, and athletic. There was more to this relationship than mutual attraction, at least from Brad Phelps, Sumi's husband.'

Niles didn't have to wait too long to find out the ties that bound this reverse princess-frog paradox.

At the initial examination by Brad's attorney, Binder Overstreet and the cross-examination by Sumi's Pakistani native co-counsel Taket Likamoni, as the re-directs of both the plaintiff and the defendant unfolded, it became very clear to Niles where their tangential lines crossed.

They had met on a private members only Internet chat/date site aimed at Asian professionals.

Brad Phelps, although not being of Asian descent, had an affinity for eastern *cuisine* of the female variety, with a preference toward Korean. Brad liked that he could count on Sumi's culturally inbred hard work ethic, extreme loyalty, and respect for male dominance.

Sumi did a stellar job in masking her not so quiet desperation in finding a suitable mate. She was not looking for an American per se, but intent on honoring her parents, whose family had suffered under the brutality of the Japanese occupation during World War II. Their only requirement was that she not bring home a Japanese man. Her mother and father were willing to help her in the process by introducing her to a reputable Korean matchmaker but Sumi respectfully declined their offer.

Having the gift of gab, Brad Phelps postured himself as being a highly successful sales manager but was really a part-time mid-level telemarketing rep working the phones just to make enough money during the day to play at night. Not that Brad didn't have the academic credentials or the right pedigree that would have predicted a higher career trajectory; he was in fact a USC grad with deep Orange County California roots.

Disappointed that college life had ended, Brad was on a mission not to let the music stop. Dropping out of grad school due to its inherent rigors, Brad simultaneously lost his major source of funding: his parents. In urgent need of a financial lifeline, serendipity graced Brad's world in the manifestation of Sumi.

If Brad was the consummate frat boy, Sumi was the polar opposite. Having worked her way through grad and post-grad school, Sumi held several advanced degrees and just as many lucrative patents. She was actually given the once in a lifetime opportunity to work on the highly coveted Human Genome Project.

What Sumi lacked in the way of classic looks, she made up for it with superabundant talent and hard work. A bit homely but not characteristically ugly, Sumi was perfect for Brad's needs, who believed he could easily control her. However, there was only one major problem to overcome: to possess her would necessitate marrying her.

Never having dated throughout her school years and beyond, Sumi could not believe that this gorgeous man had actually paid her the time of day. Having grown up in a very strict religious family that forbade premarital sex, Brad was her first.

This was not a big impediment for Brad, he knew he could trust Sumi. And being the liberal minded person he was, he never intended to declare a self-imposed moratorium on random encounters with equally liberated women post marriage. That, plus the fact that Sumi never even batted an eye when Brad declared that he had decided to quit work to pursue his lifelong dream of becoming a professional volleyball player. Although far too old to be seriously considered, he actually had tried to qualify for the ATP Tour.

From the courtroom banter, it was evident that Sumi had suspected that her husband was not completely faithful, but being a non-confrontational person she just retreated into her work. This pseudo-marriage of convenience came to a screeching halt when Sumi, while at a routine visit to her gynecologist, was informed that she had contracted a potent strain of the Herpes Simplex II virus. When her doctor began to query about her sexual habits and partners, Sumi was speechless, shrinking in embarrassment. All her insecurities came flooding back with a vengeance. In literal shock and in disbelief, all the scales fell from her eyes, seeing for the first time what this man was doing to her.

Although not believing in divorce, Sumi was forced to consider it. She couldn't deny that her life had drastically changed.

She was torn – who would want her now?

Should she just bury her feelings and suck it up like all the other times?

Surprisingly to everyone and not least to Sumi herself, this newfound predicament had a transforming effect on her. Instead of throwing herself a grand pity party, as would have been the bet, if one asked anybody that knew her, the situation actually made her stronger. Sumi had had enough. She was determined to take control of her life and as her African-American college roommate Toni would have said, "Kick this good for nothing man to the curb."

Sumi was quite proud of herself, feeling exhilarated by the rush of her new found boldness. But that initial euphoria wouldn't last.

After obtaining a referral to the all-female law firm of Blair, Ingram, Thatcher, Clark, Hand, Eiger, and Sloan from the Employees Assistance Program, or commonly referred to EAP, Sumi was rocked once again. She was informed that not only was she on the hook for huge alimony payments, and even though she submitted her patents while still single, the fact that they were not granted until after the wedding, they would be considered as community property since they were filed in her married name.

She never had even considered a prenuptial agreement, thinking that it would cast a shadow over what God had finally blessed her with and thereby possibly scare away her Adonis fiancé.

However this fact would not escape the keen eyes of the renowned "forensic accountants" at Green, Richards, Eiseman, Ernst, and Dunn, the firm hired by her golden boy and soon to be ex-husband.

Brad would without a doubt get what Sumi would eventually have to pay.

As Niles absorbed all the salacious details of this gender bending of socially normative roles, he had to admit that this case was challenging his notions of conventional wisdom with respect to his assumptions about victims and perpetrators. He had only heard tales of able-bodied men taking advantage of hard working women; but now, he was seeing it, up close and personal. Instead of feeling a tinge of glee with the tables finally being turned, Niles was disgusted. From his standpoint, this was compelling evidence that the pendulum had swung too far.

It was not enough that this woman was getting treated the same unfair way historically reserved for men; it proved that the system was out of control.

But the immediate question was: is Sumi a candidate?

3

It was puzzling. The invitation contained only a secure ID token with an encrypted password, and an auto-load web address.

Sumi thought it was just another clever marketing idea from a vendor trying to slickly capture her attention.

It worked.

After inserting the device into her computer's USB port and running a virus scan, Sumi was startled at what appeared on the screen.

Rather than a solicitation from a vendor it was much more personal.

The question on the screen read:

"DO YOU BELIEVE THIS LIFE IS FAIR?"

"What the hell?" raced through the neural pathways of her frontal lobe before this question escaped her throat.

~

Sumi's senses were assaulted again by the blaring sound of *"Black Dog"* piercing her ears by the lead guitar of Led Zeppelin. This was coming from the ringtone on her cell, courtesy of her clandestine project partner Zeke.

Startled, Sumi fumbled through her purse and tapped the liquid crystal display of her recently purchased Blackberry KEYone Smart Phone, (just introduced by the company formerly known as RIM in an attempt to rejuvenate the fortunes of the now ailing but once a tech giant).

Exasperated, Sumi exhaled into the phone. "Zeke, I know this is your dime but could you please let me know how I can change this insane ringtone? It's driving me crazy!"

"Ah yeah well you really don't want to do that."

"Why?"

"When I programmed your phone, I encrypted it with a beta version of a new, unreleased supercharged 254 byte encryption utility that is really cool, you know, the best on the planet but it has a little flaw."

"Flaw? What are you talking about Zeke?"

"I wanted you to think of me every time Zeppelin played but if you don't want that, to delete my special ringtone you'd have to change the entire chip and that would wipe out all the memory – including all the apps."

"You're kidding? Zeke, tell me you are joking."

"I'm not."

"I can't believe this."

"Look on the bright side."

"Brightside? What bright side?"

"Well, if you keep me on your ringtone, you'll never lose your data and you'll never lose me."

"Sounds like a Faustian bargain."

"A what?"

"Never mind. I'm in the middle of…What did you call for?"

"Come on, Sumi, don't be pissed. Besides, I have some very interesting news."

"Can it wait? We still on for our regular time on Thursday?"

"I can't wait. You're going to want to hear this."

"Alright, alright, just cut to the chase."

"I'm ready to go live with *"Slave Driver!"* Isn't that fan- freaking-tastic?"

Slave Driver was Zeke's life's work. He had conceived and developed a multi-platform automorphic cyber-worm called a web inoculator. This program allowed one to link powerful but idle computers all around the world to crunch complex data. Unlike its menacing cousin, the "computer virus," the inoculator was designed with strict adherence to the principal clause of the Hippocratic Oath: "First do no harm."

It did not do any damage to the host computer and left no digital fingerprint to trace; its only purpose was to harness and leverage by way of a daisy-chain network, the quantum but idle computing power needed for programs that required trillions of simultaneous calculations.

"Isn't that illegal, like computer hacking?"

"Abso-freaking-lutely not! Actually…I'm hurt that you would insult me by comparing me to some low-life couch potato hacker!"

"Don't get so melodramatic, Zeke."

"Slave Driver is revolutionary. First of all, it does not spy on, nor steal, or damage anything or install cookies. In fact, as the world's first virus inoculator, it prevents hackers from trespassing by permanently closing doors behind it. I'm talking hermetically sealed here. It's a computer program that has manners! Its sole use and purpose is to put to use wasted or underutilized computing power to help solve some major analytical hurdles."

"Semantics."

"You won't be saying that when we run the Beta Test of ADEP. I don't know if you even know what that stands for."

"Enlighten me."

"Advanced DNA Extrapolator Program."

"The moment of truth. Are you sure there is no other way to get this done?"

"Not in our lifetime, Sweetie."

After having worked on the Human Genome Project, Sumi had applied for and received a patent for a breakthrough DNA sequencing process that digitized the entire strand of molecules and applied algorithmic extrapolation techniques to the alleles on chromosomes to project what the likely probabilities of what a person would look like in ten, twenty, thirty, forty years, etc.

Although hailed by the scientific community as a brilliant theory, she had yet to prove the viability and accuracy of the model due to the multiple billions of random possibilities.

Zeke informed her, "There is only one single computer that is up to the task: the IBM Sequoia Super Computer installed at the Lawrence Livermore Labs. Sequoia has the potential of processing 20 Petra-Flops of data per second. Its computing power is the equivalent to all the people on earth using calculators, non-stop for an entire year. At this rate it would take three hundred and twenty years for them to do what Sequoia could do in an hour! The only problem is that Sequoia is sequestered."

Being a renegade, Zeke opted to go rouge and "borrow" non-government assets.

Although she had serious reservations about using borrowed computer power, the potential applications could be endless – and considerably valuable.

Resigned to these realities, Sumi sighed "I guess this will have to be a conundrum for the Ethicists to solve."

"Those nuns should be shot for what they did to you good Catholic girls! Doing wrong for the right reasons is ethical as often as not."

"That conundrum aside, what are our next steps?"

"You just have to pick a subject so we can run their DNA through ADEP."

"Okay, give me a little time," looking at the blinking icon on her screen. Sumi absently asked, "By the way, have you heard of site called 'Deuxoverlife .com?'"

Max Deveraux

4

Sitting in a worn out and creaky chair in his cramped second floor office overlooking the "triangle" that linked the South Campus with the North of UCLA, Niles was busy reading and answering his emails; some of which had aged to the point of virtually growing mold.

Surviving all the budget cuts, the creature comforts in the life of a university professor were anything but luxurious but being in the elite of academia definetely had its benefits. In fact, if it were not for the recent moratorium preventing what had long been one of teaching's biggest perquisites that of turning a blind eye to the staff, dating, adult but vulnerable co-eds, this could arguably be one of the sweetest gigs around.

This change in policy had Niles seriously questioning his career choices.

Ironically, he was initially going to follow the family business in the practice of law. After arriving in Los Angeles during his undergraduate studies, he actually double majored in law and psychology.

The middle son of a French Canadian Jewish couple, Niles was confused as to which path of study he wanted to pursue in college. He was torn between following his father, a noted Quebec Scholar and Law Professor, and his now deceased mom, a Behavioral Psychologist whom he greatly admired.

When his mom died just prior to Niles' grad school, the choice became obvious and as a tribute to her, he decided on psychology with a legal twist.

What most people did not realize, even those who cried foul because of the ever increasing tuition fees, was that most of the escalating costs of college went to retain the services of the highly demanded and talented PhD's.

Truth be told, the universities in the upper echelon of higher education were engaged in a no holds barred talent war with private industry.

Niles, feeling quite buoyant, was pleased that for the most part, his selection process was going along better than expected. The only candidate that had not as of yet accepted the invitation was Sumi Kim, yet he felt confident enough that she would come around soon.

Phase II was to begin.

Niles knew this part could be tricky. But first, it was time for what most serious researchers dreaded: office hours. The time of the week when professors had to subject themselves to the insufferable questions and overt flirtations of struggling and extremely paranoid undergraduates. Students' panic was driven by the fear that if their thesis didn't pass the course with a minimum of an "A," their lives would be banished to hell, and all their fears of not making it in the real world would rush in on them like the buzz-kill that comes from getting pulled over for a DUI.

Niles sighed as he spun his chair around to the smiling and angelic face of Tiffany Lane.

Tiffany was anything but the typical over-achieving student. She was not only, brilliant, but confident, self-assured, and inquisitive. She had a personality that made one think that she not only already knew the answer to the question she posed but was at least three steps ahead of everyone else. One could visibly see, if not perceive on a meta-sensory level that her overt humility was a contrived artifact designed to disguise her superior intellect just to make one feel comfortable with oneself. The only flaw she had, if it could be called that, was that with her tall, svelte, athletic body and piercing green eyes set against her long luxuriant sable hair, she was hard to look at – and at the same time, impossible for one to take one's eyes off her, long enough to pay attention to what she was saying.

Niles suspected that her beauty would prove to be a serious distraction in the classroom should she decide to teach. No denying it, Tiffany had the whole package, and Niles was elated that she accepted his invitation to become his PhD candidate.

"Hello Professor."

"I thought we agreed for you to call me Niles?"

"Right, Dr. Niles, I had a question about this morning lecture."

"Shoot."

"You challenged the idea that rape was largely an act of power and aggression, but could it instead be possibly explained, from an evolutionary and biological perspective as an alternative yet deviant mating strategy for those who fail to obtain a mate through normal means."

"Go on."

"I was wondering how this alternative mating strategy theory could explain date rape?"

"What do you mean?" Niles was intrigued by her inquisitive mind.

"Well, by definition, date rape assumes that the perpetrator and the victim are acquainted. Correct?"

"I'm listening."

"If that assumption holds true, then the perp uses traditional means to initiate the mating process prior to employing force to subjugate his victim. Therefore, a power dynamic seems to better explain the dramatic change in behavior."

"As always, Tiffany, your reasoning is very solid; however, power alone does not explain motivation. The end result comes back to sex."

"I see, so when there is an asymmetrical balance of power in the beginning, a rapist is not attempting to obtain additional power but he is flexing his innate power by an act of aggression to obtain sex. Hmm?"

"Exactly. It wasn't until the 1970s that the issue of rape became seen as an act of power. Before that, it was generally viewed as an unlawful sex act. The sponsor for the change admitted later that although she agreed that it was about sex, the concept of power had to be introduced in order to promote the act from a misdemeanor to a felony."

"Clever. I can understand why she did it, but I also can see how by redefining it on the basis of power it could be then used to support a feminist agenda in the age-old war of the sexes."

"Precisely. As ominous as the term power in this context has become, there is really nothing new or special about it. Women use sex as power over men and men use power to obtain sex from women. It's a tool, a utility."

"Cool. Thanks for clarifying my questions. However, my real reason for coming in to see you is to bring you up to date on the data gathering for my thesis project.

"I obtained all the statistics from the Department Of Justice on violent acts committed by disgruntled spouses; I also was able to obtain divorce statistics from all fifty states.

"The American Bar Association was very helpful in providing the specific numbers regarding the increase of family-law attorneys with a divorce specialty and a fairly close estimate of the rise of legal fees in such cases.

"*The Journal of Family Law* recently published a study about how the average time it takes to settle a typical divorce has increased over the last ten year period.

"It's taken a while, but I believe that I have most of what I need from a statistical standpoint and I am now ready to build my preliminary ANOVA statistical program model along with the step-wise regression parameters," explained Tiffany.

"Great! Let's meet up in the lab later and go over the project milestones, and I can bring you up to date on the Deuxoverlife.com community I've been developing. Then we can discuss how the therapy sessions will be conducted."

"Professor, I mean Dr. Niles, since my intended work will be more akin to an observational study, isn't it a bit overreaching to call it 'therapy sessions?'"

"Touché! Let's compromise and call it 'group interaction.' And by the way, Niles is my first name."

"Sure, Dr. Niles."

Later that evening while Niles and Tiffany were working in the lab, they shared an eggplant pizza with anchovies. Niles thought he was in third heaven when Tiffany actually liked his favorite but unpopular toppings.

As the two labored on their respective parts of the project, they sought input from each other. Tiffany was furiously imputing data into the MINITAB statistical program on her computer.

Interrupted by Niles, heaving an exhausted sigh, moaned, "Okay Tif', now it's your turn."

Tiffany, turning in her small swivel chair, glanced momentarily at the words painted in capital letters on the wall above Niles' desk, which read:

- THE PhD CREDO: PUBLISH OR PERISH -

"My turn for what?" she asked.

"To create your Avatar."

"My what?"

"Your Avatar. It's your virtual personality in Deuxoverlife.com. It's really cool…come here and take a look."

Rolling her swivel chair across the floor to his right side, Tiffany was confused at first but then her expression changed to one of amusement as she looked at the animated figures on the thirty-six inch Apple monitor.

"This is what everyone has been talking about? It looks like some kind of kids' game."

"It's not. Granted, it may look like a video game but it's far from that. Deuxoverlife.com is a very powerful online virtual world. Anything you do in real life can be done within Deuxoverlife.com.

"For example, you can set up a business, like a clothing store, sell products and make real money. You can organize political campaigns, set up charity events, have corporate meetings, set up dates, start a band and become a rock star or visit anywhere, any place on earth, learn about people and different cultures. And yes, you can also play games!"

He paused for a minute to reflect, then Professor Niles went on, "But one of the most powerful uses of Deuxoverlife.com is the ability to organize specialized community groups – and for our purposes, the ability to arrange Group Interaction Sessions for the people we select who have been severely wronged by the judicial system and as a result may have developed homicidal ideations. The beauty of Deuxoverlife.com is in its anonymity – how it allows participants to recreate themselves in any way they want."

He gathered his thoughts, "For example: let's say that in real life you are a janitor but you really want to be a surgeon. You can create that personality by setting up your own clinic and performing online plastic surgery. However, I would suggest that if you choose that occupation for yourself, Tiffany, you might consider getting as much virtual malpractice insurance you can afford!"

Tiffany replied, "So you mean to tell me, you can create any personality and/or identity you want and interact with other virtual people just like you do on a daily basis?"

"Yes, and then some. You would be surprised how many people would love to give birth to their alter ego with impunity. While it's true that you can do virtually anything you want in this platform, it's not without risk."

"What do you mean?"

"Well, let's say that if someone is not well-adjusted in real life, there is nothing preventing him or her from carrying those same personality flaws into Deuxoverlife.com. For example if you were a conman in real life there is a likely chance that you will do the same thing or worse in Deuxoverlife.com. At the extreme end of the spectrum, a rapist could become a serial rapist in the virtual world. There are really very few limitations. The most attractive thing, and also the scariest thing, is its absolute anonymity."

"Sounds highly compelling Professor Niles, but I can see how it can get out of control."

"The premise of the site, is that control, is for the real world."

"I understand."

"In an intriguing way, this raw untamed world could serve our research purposes perfectly, insofar as our participants may be less inhibited and reveal not only who they really aspire to be, but provide insights into their psyche and the emotional triggers that precede actionable behaviors including violence. They can do all this under the cover of anonymity and reveal their id with impunity."

"Deep. But potentially dangerous given the lack of controls on individual behavior."

"Possibly."

"Okay, where do I start?" Tiffany asked excitedly.

"Step one is picking a gender with all the attendant physical accoutrements; step two is picking your new occupation or vocation as the case may be. Following that, you can go shopping for clothing, a car and building an online resume; and finally, selecting and joining groups and associations you are interested in or actually creating one of your own. Here is a temporary password and ID along with a bank account to purchase your basics to 'go live.'"

"I know exactly who I want to be."

"This is an anonymous procedure. I'll step outside."

"I'm your PhD candidate, Dr. Niles." She smiled. "You're welcome to observe."

Niles leaned over Tiffany's right shoulder to watch her build her online persona. He was careful not to betray his intense pleasure as he voyeuristically observed her knowing fingers vigorously attacking the keyboard.

The 42 year-old Professor was indeed handsome. His 6'1" frame supported his athletic build. Niles' fairly long reddish-blond mane frequently caught the attention of fellow female staff members and coeds alike. Although he was not vain, Tiffany's apparent indifference continued to puzzle him.

"Okay, I'm done."

"You're serious?"

"Um hum."

"Your alter-ego is a football player?"

"You said that in Deuxoverlife.com I would have the freedom to be whoever I wanted to be. I have always wanted to know what it would feel like to be a male butthole and it seems to me that those who most exemplify this have got to be jocks and I should know since I've dated enough of them!"

"This ought to be fun..." said Niles overenthusiastically.

"Welcome to my world," Tiffany said, with a coy smile.

Over the next few hours Niles and Tiffany went over the detailed research protocols and organization of the five planned sessions.

As expected, Tiffany made the major contributions to key program design elements. Niles was very impressed, and truly relieved that he wouldn't have to carry the whole load on this one. Their combined enthusiasm served as fuel to push the academic envelop, and the possible potential social impacts that this cutting-edge research could have on the scientific advancement in understanding the relationship between the law and human behavior. Putting aside their professional bias – that the laws, one lives by, have not kept pace with the way one actually lives – Niles and Tiffany realized that heuristically speaking, they were embarking on some very important work. Simultaneously, they both shared an unspoken sense that they were really on to something significant, which made Nobel thinkable and honorariums a foregone conclusion.

5

After leaving her attorney's downtown office, Sumi drove eight miles to a pharmacy in the nearby town of Downey, hoping that she would be unnoticed as she filled her Valtrex prescription.

Overwhelmed with disillusionment, Sumi could not shake the deep sense of emptiness she felt as she reflected on the dramatic and unexpected changes in her life. She could handle the cheating, and given what her mom had to deal with; Sumi had assumed that this was what men did. But what really shook her to the core, was the question, 'What did I do to deserve being treated so insignificantly?'

'MY GOD, HERPES!' the words echoed, loud and clear, in her head, as she had to abruptly swerve back into her lane, momentarily losing her awareness.

It was impossible for her to reconcile what Brad had done to her, and the fact that she now was ordered to pay him spousal support and share the royalties of her patents; something that he had absolutely nothing to do with. It made her quake with anger and disgust.

Sumi realized that she could not go through this process alone. She concluded that she would avail herself of the strange invitation to participate in the online group interaction sessions at Deuxoverlife.com. After all, what could she possibly lose? Since it was all virtual, no one would know who she really was. All she had to do was be clever in the selection of her Avatar.

Paranoid, Sumi sat in the car and as she waited in the parking lot scanning for familiar faces going in and out of the pharmacy. Taking a deep breath, she hesitantly ventured out of the vehicle and darn near ran into the entrance, hoping that her dark glasses and headscarf would be enough not to betray her identity. Although, she didn't know anyone who actually lived in Downey, Sumi could have sworn that the girl at the counter was someone she had seen before.

Realizing that she was just tripping, Sumi was relieved when she was back in her car and on her way home.

'Thank God that's over,' she thought, grateful that she had been given a six-month prescription; she was determined to use the Internet to fulfill her next one.

During the ride home, Sumi distracted herself from her personal problems by focusing on the conversation that she and Zeke had shared. Sumi sensed that Zeke, for all his quirkiness and thinly veiled crush on her, was really a brilliant computer genius.

A smile slowly formed on her lips as she amusingly thought about how Zeke seriously thought he was being watched by some Orwellian Big Brother!

"Come on Zeke, get real," she would giggled at him. "The FBI, CIA, MI-6, Mossad? Really? I'm sure they have other more important things to do than listen in on some hermit bunkered down in his basement."

'Oh well, Zeke is just being Zeke,' she thought.

At any other time, Sumi would have been thrilled that the ADEP beta was ready to be tested. But right now, she was scared. The real issue was going to be finding a suitable subject who would pass the peer scrutiny that was sure to come.

Slipping on her Bluetooth earpiece, Sumi tapped the voice command button on her Blackberry and placed a call to Zeke.

Getting his antiquated answering machine, a frustrated Sumi said, "Zeke, if you haven't been arrested by Homeland Security or the NSA, please pick up the dang phone!"

After verifying Sumi's voice, Zeke picked up.

"Hey Sumi, what's crackin'?"

"Must you always do that when I call?"

"What?"

"Let it go to your answering machine."

"How many times do I have to tell you, incoming calls don't just go to the answering machine, they go through my voice recognition software?"

"But you have caller ID!"

"You can never be too careful, anyone could have snatched your phone and pretended to be you."

"Whatever. Listen…"

"Shoot."

"How long did you say it would take to run the ADEP program to get the final imaging clear enough for recognition?"

"Well, that's a complicated question. Let's see …in order to get high def at the 1080i level, it's going to take a long time."

"How long is long?"

"Hard to say."

"Your best guess."

"Sumi, we're talking serious computing here. This is not something that can be rushed."

"Just ballpark it."

"There are too many variables in play."

"Like what?"

"Like how much excess capacity can we harness, and since we can only use it when the computers are supposed to be dark, we can only get so much power per day. Conceivably, since we can only expect one line of pixels per run, it could take weeks or more."

"I had no idea it would take that long," said Sumi, disappointed.

Zeke, detecting this, continued explaining, "For what we're doing, that's lightning speed. Remember, this is the beta round. We don't have any certainty that it will ultimately function properly and what bugs we are going to have to work out. This is beyond rocket science; it's the real deal! Sumi dear, we are on to some NEXT LEVEL STUFF! You can't microwave this kind of 'evo-revo-lutionary' stuff, no way!"

"I suppose your right."

"And the longer you wait to pick the subject the longer it's going to take."

"I'm not dragging my feet here Zeke, it's just that I would also like to demonstrate a practical and urgent application along with showcasing the viability of the program taking it out of the theoretical stage."

"Why is that important?"

"Just think of the potential applications? Law enforcement, kidnapping, medicine, disease prevention ..."

"How about dating?"

"Dating?"

"Yeah, dating. Just think, if you meet someone and god forbid think about marriage, you could run ADEP on your girlfriend and if you don't like what you are going to see in twenty or thirty years, you can get out of Dodge now and skip the divorce proceedings."

"You're crazy!"

"I betcha' if this was around thirty years ago there would be a lot less fatherless babies born! In fact, I think it will make a significant contribution to actually lowering the divorce rate. It will take the guesswork out of the equation, pun intended!"

"I confess, that is one application I never really thought about," said Sumi.

"Well that's why they pay you and not me the big bucks."

Sumi laughed, "They will be running to you for high-cost research once this goes epic, Zeke, so get it ready!"

6

Exhilarated by her Saturday morning routine run through Runyon Canyon, Tiffany grabbed a large cup of her favorite Columbian coffee and indulged herself with one of her guilty pleasures – a cheese Danish from Café Champaign on her way to the lab.

She wanted to get an early start on completing all the data input before she was to meet with Niles later that afternoon. Tiffany was excited by the prospect that she would be able to get a sneak peek at the preliminary statistical output. She was hopeful, she would discover that the correlational relationship between spousalcide and adverse judgment would be confirmed. However, she understood that proving a causal relationship would require a more robust analysis. Either way, she was confident that her doctoral dissertation would be groundbreaking, and at the very least, instigate a reassessment of the notion of so-called "No Fault" divorce statutes.

Motivated by her own family tragedy, Tiffany had debated early in her academic career whether to pursue law or veterinary medicine. While she was still in middle school, the deciding factor was the nagging question of "Why?" Why was her much-beloved older sister viciously murdered by her estranged husband? It took many years of counseling before she was able to harness the coping tools that allowed her to function. If it were not for her strenuous exercise regime that subsequently led to an athletic scholarship.

Finishing the step-wise regression, Tiffany gained a directional indicator to where her research was headed but she still needed Niles' input to help interpret the inferences.

After popping into the UCLA food court to get a quick lunch, consisting of a fruit-bowl and a power bar, Tiffany met up with a visibly buoyant Niles back in the lab.

"Great news," he bellowed.

"I have some interesting news of my own, but you first."

"Our last participant has signed up and we're ready to go!"

"That's wonderful, Dr. Niles!"

"Sure is!"

"That trumps mine, but we can deal with that later."

"Alright then, what we need to do now is go over the background profiles we developed from the questionnaires and family court observations of each participant."

"That ought'a be fun!"

"It's only fitting that from the List, we start with Sumi. After all, isn't it said that, "the first shall be last and the last shall be first?""

"Where does it say that?"

"Not sure, it just sounds right."

"Whatever."

Niles had been debriefing Tiffany on a weekly basis. She was already somewhat familiar with Sumi's background, and as Niles filled in the blanks, the pair was able to review the profiles and court fact sheets on each candidate starting with Sumi's.

SUMI K.

AGE: *39.*

OCCUPATION: *Geneticist.*

EDUCATION: *Multiple PhD's.*

INCOME: *Higher Wage Earning Spouse.*

MARITAL HISTORY: *First Marriage, 7 years.*

CHILDREN: *Childless.*

COURT STATUS: *Respondent.*

JUDGEMENT: *Court ordered spousal support and share of future value of patent royalties.*

AVATAR: *Super Model (SM).*

NOTES: *-None-.*

7

KYLE S.
AGE: *31.*
OCCUPATION: *Sanitation Worker.*
EDUCATION: *GED.*
INCOME: *Not Contested.*
MARITAL HISTORY: *Married 6 years.*
CHILDREN: *No Biological Offspring.*
COURT STATUS: *Respondent.*
JUDGEMENT: *Settled outside of court and agreed to pay spousal support and share retirement benefits and provide medical insurance for 3 years.*
AVATAR: *Hockey Player (HP).*
NOTES: *-None-.*

Everything was going well and seemed to be getting even better for Kyle. Despite a rough and tumbled childhood, and requisite minor run-ins with the law, Kyle had managed to turn his life around. He entered a work-study program that led him to getting his GED. After finishing the Operating Engineer Apprenticeship Program, he landed a good paying job with the County of Los Angeles, complete with a full benefits package including medical and dental. Since the job was a governmental entity, he also qualified for a 457B /TSA plan.

Kyle loved his job, and loved even more the smile his success had put on his mom's face.

After years of cruising the bar scene and doing some serious damage with the ladies, Kyle yielded to the yearnings of his mom and began to think seriously about starting a family of his own.

Kyle might not have been a genius in the classroom, but he was smart enough to know that the woman for him was not going to be one of the fillies he would meet, hit and quit at the club. No, he was going to take his time to pick the right one.

Growing impatient with her favorite son, Kyle's mom, Lydia, suggested that he try one of the online dating services. Kyle's protest did not deter Lydia one bit. Although she had very little direct knowledge of the Internet, she did know that her cousin's daughter had found her husband on a dating site and was now pregnant with her second child.

Not wanting to disappoint his mom, Kyle relented and opened an account with eHarmony.com.

This online dating service was different from others such as Match.com, which based their matches on the theories of the daughter and mom team of sociologists who believed that opposites attract.

The Myers-Briggs color coded personality mapping system of Yellow, Blue, Green and Red was a complimentary model, which suggested that certain weaknesses in one person could be matched with certain strengths in another person, and vice versa. Ergo, they would not compete with each other and hence reduce conflict.

Match.com's model was indeed the linear opposite of the eHarmony's complementary theory.

Mr. Warren, the founder of eHarmony, based his matching system on the theory that the best chance at matrimonial/relational harmony was the idea that likeminded people tend to want the same things. They are therefore better suited for each other, and would have to make fewer adjustments in their relationships. This theory oscillated around twenty-nine critical dimensions of compatibility.

Since both methodologies were proprietary and because the whole online dating industry was still in its relative infancy, there had been few, if any independent scientific studies to validate or compare, which system yielded the best results.

Kyle was sold on the notion that by definition, likenesses were better than differences. If he had only known then what that notion foreshadowed.

Nevertheless, eHarmony was his clear choice.

After getting and receiving about one hundred winks and emails, Kyle was thrilled when he saw the picture of Teri.

Reading her profile, he had that unexplainable feeling (what the French call "je ne sais quoi") of knowing or hoping as the case maybe, rushed over him like the spray over the bow of a raft going down a level-5 rapid.

If Teri was anything close to what her profile claimed and her picture showed, this could be the start of some real fun!

When Teri hit him back with a light-hearted email asking him what he thought about the prospect of the LA Kings making it to the Stanley Cup Playoffs? To say he was impressed with this; was a mild understatement. Kyle finally met a girl who loved sports as much as he did.

After numerous email and text message exchanges, they agreed to meet and both their worlds changed. The more they talked the more they were convinced that this was a once in a lifetime chance to find real companionship and love.

eHarmony led to a friendship, friendship led to fun, fun led to commitment and to Kyle's mother's delight, it eventually led to marriage.

Kyle and Teri decided that they would spend the first few years collecting memories by taking sports vacations, visiting as many historic baseball, football and basketball stadiums as possible, before they started their family.

Kyle was so happy that his athletic and sports loving wife liked the same things he did.

After many frustrating years of trying, Teri wasn't getting pregnant.

Not understanding what the problem was, Kyle began to wonder if it might be him. Could he, like his uncle, be sterile…or maybe suffering from a low sperm count?

One day by chance, while trying to fill out insurance information for his annual benefits open enrollment period, Kyle stumbled upon some of Teri's old medical records.

His wife had told him about the small ovarian cyst that she had removed. Oddly on the questionnaire, she had checked off the box for testicular cancer instead of the one for ovarian cancer.

Weird mistake! Thinking it was just that, in a kidding sort of way, he casually asked Teri about it. Expecting her to laugh with him, he was shocked when Teri broke out in tears.

Thinking it was some sort of female hormonal thing, he tried to console his wife, telling her that he was just kidding and it was no big deal. After a while, Teri gained her composure and asked him if he truly loved her. Patiently, Kyle assured his wife of his love and commitment. Choking back tears, Teri slowly and meanderingly told Kyle of her confusion as a child and how she tried to cope with intense internal struggles with her identity.

After a few gut-wrenching hours, she revealed that, "yes", it was true she was diagnosed with testicular cancer and after living as a female for two years, at age twenty-three, she underwent complete sexual reassignment surgery. Teri went on to tell Kyle that she wanted to tell him from the very beginning, but could not risk losing what she felt was "true love." She had hoped that over time, as their love grew, he would accept her for who she was…

And ultimately, they could always adopt.

Visibly upset, Kyle blew out of the house, unable to say a word. After retching in the front yard, he wobbled to his late model Dodge Ram sports utility truck and went on a drive, which eventually ended up at his mother's home. Unable to talk to her that night, he just went upstairs to his old room and tried unsuccessfully to fall asleep.

Kyle missed work the next two days. Finally, he decided to tell his mom Lydia what had happened. He'd never seen such a look of shock on his mother's face.

He quietly decided to petition for a divorce. He did not want anyone, especially his friends and co-workers to find out what had happened.

He was going to keep this secret.

Any notion of this vanished when Teri contested the spousal support issues in court. Teri, or Terry as was her/his given name, under the advisement of her lawyer, as a tactical move, threatened to go public with the news of her gender change knowing this would compel Kyle to settle, even though he was the victim of her deceit.

Teri and her lawyer assumed correctly.

Despite Kyle's extreme if not justified anger, he wanted to move on with what was left of his shattered life. A drawn-out court battle would reveal everything and this was indeed the last thing he wanted.

Kyle was now on the hook for 40% of his gross income, had to provide health insurance for three years and since she was vested in his retirement plans, he also had to share this as well as a part of his future Social Security payments.

8

MIKKI B.
AGE: *43.*
OCCUPATION: *Unemployed former Women's High School Basketball coach.*
EDUCATION: *Bachelor of Arts, Physical Education.*
INCOME: *Sole Wage Earner.*
MARITAL HISTORY: *Not Married.*
CHILDREN: *Adopted Daughter of Partner Jo.*
COURT STATUS: *Respondent.*
JUDGEMENT: *Ordered to surrender house and continue child support. No visitation rights due to alleged (by Josephina Delgado, her ex-partner) statutory rape of female player, further ordered to register as sex offender.*
AVATAR: *Amazon (AMZ).*

NOTES: *They met in 2008 at a late night rally on Sunset Boulevard in support of the overturn of California's infamous Proposition 8. The voters approved ban on same sex marriage.*

Mikki and Jo shared a deep passion of hate for the hypocritical Christian Right.

Both could not believe that California, of all places, would send civil rights hurling back into the stone ages. It was simply preposterous!

The real cause behind the voter approved defeat was not morality, because poll after poll showed that most Californians didn't care about who married who – it was all about voter turnout.

Since the issue didn't affect the majority, they simply didn't inconvenience themselves to show up at the voting booths. The real reason for Prop 8's persistence was and has always been that low voter turnout; always favoring the conservatives.

Although it got fewer headlines, the real battle for LGBTQ (Lesbian, Gay, Bisexual, Transgender and Queer) rights was not against their opponents – it was with their fair-weather friends, who professed their undying liberal-minded support over beers at the sports bars but never showed up for the game nor the poll booths.

Proposition 8 was a clear evidence of the political phenomena called the Bradley Effect, where the polls showed strong support but those supporters just did not show up at the booths.

Ironically, Mikki and Jo owed their union to a cause designed to keep them apart.

With Mikki living in Los Angeles and coaching girls' basketball at Fairfax High, while Jo and her daughter lived in Ventura County with Jo's mother; came the predictable longings, stresses and strains of being apart. After almost a year of struggling with this somewhat long distance relationship, at least from a driving standpoint, at Jo's urging and Mikki's reservetions, they decided to move in together, in Mikki's house in West Hollywood.

The couple began settling in as a family, and delightfully, Jo's daughter Amber developed a very close and effortless relationship with both women. So close that when Jo suggested the idea of Mikki adopting Amber formally as co-parent, it all seemed perfectly natural. They did accomplish this, and none happier about it than Amber. She was proud to brag to the other kids at school that she had two moms!

Mikki enjoyed how Jo took such an interest in her work. The fact that she was so genuinely intrigued by the details, backgrounds and personalities of the players on Mikki's team, created an unexpected bond between them.

Over time, however, the tenor of Jo's inquires caused Mikki to detect a slight edge to some of her partner's questions. Although she didn't voice it, Jo seemed to be having some difficulties as she learned more about the life of a specific top-rated basketball player.

Sure there were a lot of games and meetings, but what Jo struggled with, was how much more there was to coaching especially off the court. She did not seem to understand how much Mikki had to deal with the personal lives of the players. If a player was distracted by outside issues, it was sure to show-up at some point, on the court. And some players needed more hand-holding then others. It was only natural that some would look to the leadership of their coach to help with problems that parents would or could not deal with.

Things began to heat up right before the CIF tournament. Jo knew that Mikki's goal, in running one of the top high school female basketball programs in the country, was very ambitious.

And that she eventually wanted to become a head coach at Division I College team. Jo heard Mikki repeatedly mention how great it would be to have a chance to interview for the top spot at Tennessee, the University of Connecticut or Stanford.

Mikki could not understand why Jo was making such a big deal about spending so much time with Sara Thompson, her star center.

Mikki knew that Sara was going to be her ticket to "The Show."

Mikki and Sara wanted their relationship to reach a deeper level of commitment. They were very close and made sure to spend a great deal of time together. They always felt that their futures inextricably intertwined with each other.

Unable to constrain her insecurities, Jo's questions about Mikki and Sara, became borderline accusations of impropriety between the two basketball addicts.

At first Mikki just brushed this off as being silly but no matter how much she reassured Jo of her commitment to her and Amber, it was becoming clear that there would always be some jealous subtext to their conversations.

When Mikki saw the post-it-note on her desk requesting that she meet with the Athletic Director at 3:00 pm, she assumed that it was in response to the article in the paper that mentioned her name along with a few others in regard to a possible vacancy at Baylor – not her first choice but a top ten program nonetheless. Mikki casually read the scouting report outside of the director's office for the upcoming tournament.

She was finally ushered in to the Director's office. She took a seat across from the director.

John, a former men's basketball star, was tall, silver haired and very attractive for a man his age. As the two caught each other's glance, Mikki was a little unnerved by the puzzled and strange defeated look on John's face.

After a pause too long, he simply snorted, "So do you want to tell me about it?"

"About?"

"You know what I'm getting at."

"Unless you believe the rumors that I'm a mind-reader are true, you're going to have to spell it out for me."

"Why are you making this so difficult?"

"John, I don't know what the hell you are talking about, I got a team waiting for their coach."

"Alright, here goes. I just got an anonymous call about some seriously inappropriate and don't force me to elaborate, behavior between you and Sara Thompson."

Mikki was beyond shocked.

"That's a bunch of bull and you know it!"

"The caller had specific dates and times."

"What are you saying John?"

"It's not what I'm saying, it's what the press will be saying in tomorrow's paper. And it appears it was a leak from more than one source."

"John! I don't believe this!"

"Believe it, because it's going down, and I'm afraid, you with it."

"This smells like some orientation bias."

"I admit that the trustees and some of the parents had some issues with your lifestyle but you proved yourself and you've been a winner and everyone has benefited. And I can assure you, Mikki, this is not coming from within our department."

"Looks like I'm going to need to talk to my lawyer."

"You should and until this is resolved, I'm going to have to suspend you without pay. I have no choice."

It was not until her lawyer had subpoenaed the school's telephone records during discovery that Mikki found the source of the lies and distortions. The records showed that several of the numbers belonged to a Josephina Delgado.

At that moment, reality came crashing down on Mikki. It was Jo. Mikki could not believe that "her" Jo would do such a thing.

Underestimating Jo's irrational insecurities and the extreme lengths she would go to get the attention she wanted, proved to be Mikki's major oversight.

Mikki attempted to kick Jo out of the house but instead she got slapped with a restraining order.

The accusations stemming from Jo's "anony-mous tips" to the papers and the school, led to Mikki being temporally registered as a sex offender.

Consequently, not only was she prohibited from coaching girls' basketball but was also barred from seeing her own daughter Amber.

As a result of the hearings in family custody court, Mikki was ordered to pay child support. And she was also forbidden to remove Amber and by extension Jo, from their place of residence. She not only had to leave her own home but continue to pay the mortgage.

Mikki was forced to move in with her mother and father.

The publicity made it impossible for her to find work. When her savings ran out and she hit the limit on her credit cards, she had to borrow money from friends and family to meet her court ordered obligations.

9

CLAUDIA C.
AGE: 56.
OCCUPATION: *Former Congregational Church First Lady (Preacher's Wife).*
EDUCATION: *Associates of Arts Degree in Social Work.*
INCOME: *None.*
MARITAL HISTORY: *First Marriage, 12 years.*
CHILDREN: *4.*
COURT STATUS: *Plaintiff.*
JUDGEMENT: *-None-.*
AVATAR: *Avenging Angel (AA).*
NOTES: *-None-.*

Claudia sustained many emotional blows as lethal to the head, as they were to her heart.

How could she be so trusting? The many cover-ups and endless piles of forgiveness; for what? For their future, he begged, and the future of their kids.

Her soon to be ex-husband, the Right Reverend Chasen Cash, was recently defrocked and disgraced as a Pastor of a Mega Church – ironically not due to the numerous rumored infidelities, as they were considered a personal matter. What the church could not tolerate was the massive misappropriation of church funds siphonned off to finance a "wanna-be-celebrity pastor" lifestyle.

In court, the former "Pastor to the Stars" claimed no income. All of Chasen's personal assets were surreptitiously moved to his maternal family trust, safely protected from creditors as well as insulated from civil suits including those stemming from Claudia.

As head of the "Church for the Homeless Outreach Program," Claudia just kept blindly forging those checks to cover her husband's mounting debts, assured that it was all for a higher purpose. The lies, the women …hell, the men! And now, all the blame was being laid neatly at her feet. She was likened to Jezebel and Eve.

Chasen was so clever at displacing blame by distancing himself when he sensed his cover unraveling – always throwing himself on the mercy of those already deceived. Knowing that his gullible flock loved a repentant sinner, and believed that by forgiving him, they would ensure themselves eternal absolution from their own seared collective conscience.

What finally broke Claudia's spirit was when he pointed his finger at her – at his own loving wife and repository of all his pain. That "signature finger" Chasen so adroitly used when delivering his renowned and awe-inspiring sermons, was now being used as Adam pointed to Eve to mask his own moral failure.

Chasen really didn't care what happened to his wife or anyone else.

He was incapable of empathy due to his high-functioning Borderline Personality Disorder or BPD. As all BPD's, Chasen needed to be taught to respect others' personal limits but he failed in this completely.

To save himself and his ministry, Claudia was to be the Anointed One – to suffer for all of her husband's sins.

10

E. THOMAS W.
AGE: 36.
OCCUPATION: *Family Law Attorney.*
EDUCATION: *BA Economics Yale, JD Stanford. Graduated at Top of His Class.*
INCOME: *Sole Wage Earner.*
MARITAL HISTORY: *Never Married.*
CHILDREN: *None (that he knows of).*
COURT STATUS: *Respondent.*
JUDGEMENT: *Reaffirmed legality of prior consent of Asset Transfer.*
AVATAR: *Court Jester (CJ).*
NOTES: *-None-.*

As a confirmed bachelor, E. Thomas Wasserman III or ET³ as his close friends called him, played the dating field aggressively and won. That was before he met his match: a stripper named Anika, professionally known as (pka) Senserity.

With Senserity, E. Thomas, enjoyed the most intense tease he'd ever had. Eventually he was helplessly compelled to confess his undying love for her... he was obsessed! When she refused all of his gifts, money, and dates outside of the club, he viewed that as confirmation that she lived up to her name.

When she slipped to him that she was working on her Master's Degree in Psychology, being a student of human behavior and motivation himself, convinced him all the more that she was real and the one for him.

However, "working" in the atmosphere that she was in, Senserity appeared to be jaded by love. The empty promises men made to her, especially when intoxicated by her beauty.

One thing Senserity was acutely aware of was her effect she had on men. When Tom pressed her about what it would take for her to agree to an exclusive relationship, she stared into his wanting green eyes and unhesitatingly ticked off her conditions; that if a man was truly in love with her, she knew exactly what he would have to do to prove the veracity of his love before she committed.

Her requirements were few, simple and severe:

(1) She would only marry once and under no conditions would she ever consider living with a man before marriage.

(2) She would not, under any circumstances, consent to a prenuptial agreement.

(3) He would have to assign over half of his assets first as a gesture of trust and sincerity.

E. Thomas felt invincible upon news of an upcoming promotion to partner in his firm. After a year of being seduced by outrageous lap dances and deeply heartfelt telephone and text conversations that overwhelmed him, Thomas, like a bull in heat, relented and gave way to his passions.

He had to have Anika at any cost...

He decided to break the good news of his promotion to Senserity at his birthday party to be held at the club where she worked. Banking on his finely tuned intuition developed by years of analyzing his opponents' unexposed weaknesses and then capitalizing on his superior understanding of human motivation, he rolled the dice.

ET^3 was immediately rendered irreversibly convinced that the upside of possessing the essence of Senserity versus the insufferable idea of losing her to a lesser man, was worth any downside risk. His flawless intuition had always been the basis of his consistent success at ringing out disproportionately large settlements.

Thomas did as Senserity demanded.

He signed over one half of his assets including his newly constructed home in one of the choicest country clubs in western Las Vegas called Southern Highlands. Originally built as a spec home, this mega-mansion would now become their family home.

However, he could not understand why Senserity kept pushing back the date for their nuptials.

He was confused. His confusion turned into fear. His fear turned into reality.

When he begged her to tell him why, she simply replied, "Because that's what I do."

When his vivid fantasy mercilessly vanished into vapors, his mind instantly crystallized around one thought, 'He could not afford to have his superiors know of his profound stupidity.'

Any leak, and his preoccupation of making partner would be shanked like an errant extra point kick left of the uprights. He kicked himself over and over again. Should he have known? Weren't all the signs there?

It was so poetic or pathetic all at the same time.

He clearly remembered from childhood studies that the only two birthdays celebrated in the bible ended with an execution. The poetic irony was that one of them followed an exotic dancer to his end. The dance was traded for half of his kingdom, and he relented because the pleasure she generated was so intense (Mark 6:21-23).

Women's power over men does not change with the ebb of time. Same tools. Same outcomes.

'History had a vicious way of repeating itself…especially for fools like me,' he thought.

11

FAITH C.
AGE: *47.*
OCCUPATION: *Entrepreneur.*
EDUCATION: *High School, some College.*
INCOME: *Higher Wage Earning Spouse.*
MARITAL HISTORY: *Second Marriage.*
CHILDREN: *Two from Previous Relationship.*
COURT STATUS: *Plaintiff.*
JUDGEMENT: *Court order spousal support and share of acquired assets after prenuptial agreement was invalidated via technical error due to change in statute missed by former lawyer.*
AVATAR: *Sheep (SH).*
NOTES: *-None-.*

The prenuptial agreement was not her idea.

It wasn't that Faith had not thought about it…in fact given what had happened during her first divorce, she would have insisted on it anyway.

Actually, her trust and comfort with Tony deepened when he brought up the idea. He told Faith that he wanted to make sure no one and especially her, was confused about his motives. He was marrying her because he loved her and wanted to bring added joy to her life. As far as the money was concerned, it did not mean anything to him because he had his own and it never brought the happiness she had brought him.

There was no question as to whom Faith was going to represent her in the drafting and negotiating of the prenuptial agreement. Both agreed that they would give their respective counsels some guidelines, and let the lawyers hash out the details. Additionally, to motivate and discipline their lawyers to get it done expeditiously, they took the precaution of insisting on flat fees so that the process would not be dragged out and interfere with their wedding plans.

She felt safe.

Tony was by all accounts a brilliant man. He was intelligent, handsome and had a plethora of solid business ideas.

Faith thought she had hit the jackpot. She'd finally found a man that stimulated her on all levels…a man that was not intimidated by her success or independence. Her equal.

Faith had never met Tony's business partner, so when he told her things were beginning to sour between them, she immediately suggested that he do his own thing. Tony told Faith that his buy-sell agreement prevented him from using the technology the two partners had co-developed until ten years after he left the company and that neither partner was forced to buyout the other partner on separation. Since all Tony's assets were tied up in the business, he did not have the necessary capital to pursue his own projects.

Without hesitation, Faith suggested that she would fund his next venture in the form of angel capital. It took several convincing conversations before Tony relented and agreed to accept her seed money and move forward to form his new company.

Faith was not just being nice but fully understood the risk she was taking. She actually felt, she was investing shrewdly, because she had all the confidence in the world that Tony would do well. She was certain that both would reap the financial benefits when one of Tony's great ideas caught lighting in a bottle and would achieve commercial success.

After the first three failures, Faith found herself bewildered as to the dichotomy between Tony's obvious intellect and his inability to execute against his seemingly well thought out business plans. At first she just thought of the old business adage, "You win some and you lose some," but she became increasingly concerned that she was throwing good money after bad. When she suggested that perhaps she could help him with some managerial support, she was shocked by Tony's heated and negative overreaction. Thinking that she had simply threatened his male ego, Faith blew it off and let the issue subside.

Faith's first clue that things were going awry was when she asked for and received a K-1 partnership tax form. As clear as day, the numbers did not correlate. Alarms set off when Tony refused to turn over his books to her tax accountant. After she threatened to cut him off altogether, he finally relented and agreed to an audit. Her accounting firm said that all the financial statements looked in order and inquired if she wanted to save some money and have them stop there and provide a simple review or did she want a full-blown opinion letter including certification. After weighing the cost benefit analysis, Faith reluctantly authorized the certification.

The call she received from the managing partner of the audit group was not good. By the time he finished his legal disclosure that amounted to nothing more than a glorified Cover Your Ass or CYA statement, she knew that she had been duped. When the audit team sampled the account payable invoices certifying that massive fraud had taken place via phony shell corporations, Faith knew it was all over. The only thing that kept her on the north side of sanity was her repeating the refrain, "thank God for the prenup, thank god for the prenup…"

God wasn't listening.

"This is bull and tantamount to legal malpractice!" she screamed at her backpedaling lawyer.

For a moment, he really thought things were going to come to blows and that he was going to get clocked by this petite woman and soon to be former client.

Her visibly embarrassed and scared lawyer tried responding over her screeching voice, "Faith, I assure you that this has never happened before and I am going to do everything in my power to protect you."

"Protect me? Protect me? Are you f-ing serious! It was your 'protection' that got me in this mess in the first place! I don't want your protection! You and your firm are going to make me whole again or you will be going back to chasing ambulances in your five thousand dollar Armani suits and Jimmy Choo shoes!"

She could not believe that this was happening. Hadn't she taken every precaution, done what she was supposed to do?

She just about lost it when her attorney said, "There appears to be a breach in the prenuptial agreement but it's just a minor oversight."

That minor oversight turned out to be a gaff of major proportions as it gave the trial judge legal cover to render the whole agreement null and void. All of Faith's assets, including income from her other businesses were now considered community property and consequently she had to share it with Tony even though he cheated her out of millions.

It was all because of that flat fee.

That cleaver idea designed to discipline her lawyer only made things worse. Because he could not bank on long drawn out back-and-forth negotiations at the standard partner rate of $700 an hour, he kicked this "routine matter" down to a sophomore associate who forgot to check for recent updates on the governing statutes.

Faith was distraught.

Had she not already paid dearly and now this?

Her wonderful Tony was an imposter.

There was no business partner, no proprietary technology and no great ideas. There were just deception, fraud and lies.

She had been illegally scammed and now she was going to be legally fleeced.

Max Deveraux

12

WILL C.
AGE: *42*
OCCUPATION: *Insurance/Banking Executive.*
EDUCATION: *BA UCLA Economics.*
INCOME: *Single Wage Earner.*
MARITAL HISTORY: *1ˢᵗ Marriage, 18 years.*
CHILDREN: *Daughter, Not Adopted.*
COURT STATUS: *Petitioner.*
JUDGEMENT: *Pay 40% of gross income plus 30% of all bonuses for half the length of marriage (9 years), plus 50% share in all royalties and licensing fees from a post separation invention.*
AVATAR: *Rock Star (RS).*
NOTES: *-None-.*

Becoming a Christian certainly had its privileges but at times it was hard to walk the straight and narrow.

The "no sex before marriage" clause in the Christian covenant was a tough one to comply with. The promise of eternal life had an even more powerful draw.

At the early age of twenty, Will knew he was at a crossroads. He figured that since he had had success in most everything he tried, marriage should be no problem and the right thing to do.

When he met and shortly thereafter married his young wife, Robbin, he thought it was a match made in heaven. After all, they were both spiritual-minded and worshiped the same God. To him she was beautiful inside and out. And the fact that she had a five-year-old son did not deter Will in the least.

Had Will's mom still been alive, he could have depended on her guidance – whether he asked for it or not. He had been on his own since he was sixteen and was doing well for himself despite the lack of higher education. The exuberance of youth and his early success made him feel invincible.

His romantic notions of what he and his new bride could experience and accomplish in life quickly became just that: notions. Reality was not very patient. He knew within the first six months of their marriage that he was outnumbered and outdone.

Any energy left over from the constant onslaught of verbal disagreements (brought on by what would later be diagnosed as severe Pre-Menstrual Dysphoric Disorder or PMDD), was consumed by her one and only child.

Will realized he had made a big mistake.

How could he get out of it and not violate his principles? Become just like his own absentee father? Was abandonment somehow genetic?

As with every other adversity he had faced, he sucked up his feelings and worked through the pain, hoping to receive God's blessings.

For a time, he managed.

From their outward appearances, the couple looked as if they were doing well, successfully masking their daily struggles.

The incentive for tolerating this life of self-flagellation could only be understood in the context of their mutual spiritual outlook of "Sacrifice now for future happiness."

The years kept piling on...with no change.

From Will's perspective, the problem was not only about the emotional toll their relationship was taking on him, but also from their diverging goals, ambitions and commitment to responsibilities. Will was determined to live and provide a better life than he had experienced growing up. Robbin was all for that, but unwilling to contribute or make any effort toward that cause.

While Will was busy trying to make it up the corporate ladder and take care of his family both financially and spiritually, Robbin contented herself lunching with her supersized church lady friends, or aggressively hunting down any fast food joint she could find...all the while blaming Will for her rapidly increasing dress size.

Repeatedly, he would beg her to use her time more wisely, educate herself or start a career, but

Robbin would refuse, saying she didn't want to get a job because it would take time away from her doing the Lord's Work.

The ever-increasing dress size coupled with the blandest, one-directional and dissatisfying sex imaginable, left Will with an acute understanding of what Hell must be like. It wasn't that Robbin didn't like sex; actually she did, but only her way. She deemed anything novel as worldly and wholly unchristian.

One thing that could be said – she was consistent.

Robbin was always a receiver and never a giver.

Ten years later, Will found himself at another crossroads. This time however, he took the path, which he thought he would never take. He had had enough. He literally felt that he was unevenly yoked and had routinely been taken advantage of. He told Robbin that he was done – consequences be damned!

His relatives, taken fully by surprise at the separation, thought he had lost his mind and did a full-court press on him, resulting in a traumatic intervention.

It worked, but failure was only delayed.

As a condition of his return and their reconciliation, Will insisted that Robbin get a career started and pursue the completion of her education. This was to act as an insurance policy against their uncertain future.

Robbin's response to all this; she got a seasonal sales associate job and enrolled in a golf class at the local community college.

Will was dumbfounded.

She just didn't get it.

When asked how this was going to help her prepare for self-sufficiency in the event if he should ever leave, she said that she would deal with it that day when and if it came.

The day was coming as sure as the return of Christ.

One of the things, which disgusted Will, was when Robbin's friends would call the house and he would overhear her dispensing marital advice to her "client" friends. Advise that she obviously never applied to herself.

Robbin's fellow congregants, because of the sheer numerical length of their marriage, perceived her as the biblically-based, venerable and respected "aged woman".

Robbin loved the respect and adoration. But underneath the veneer, she was a lazy, gluttonous, simple-minded wastrel.

Will was sick of all this, especially her.

For many years he was consumed daily by the idea of freedom. Freedom from duty. Freedom from being taken for granted. Freedom from guilt. Freedom from bad sex. Freedom from the prison called "marriage."

Freedom from Robbin.

One evening over drinks he commiserated with his friend Alura. She patiently listened to him. Upon finishing his story he was anticipating a sympathetic response from her.

Instead she just looked at him quizzically, then said, "Wow, I would have never thought you to be so pathetic. I always perceived you to be a leader and a powerful man, but what do I know?"

He couldn't feel the sting of her words, but what he heard was another voice that startled him. It was not a strong voice at all; it was wimpish…weak.

Nonetheless, it was his voice.

An internal voice that demanded attention.

It was as if he had heard it for the first time. Embarrassed, Will let out a self-conscious laugh, realizing that he had turned into the proverbial sissy.

The next morning as he got in his car, he said "F' it," and drove straight to "We the People," the legal document preparer to get the divorce paperwork started.

He felt empowered. He felt exhilarated.

At the same time he wanted to keep the lid on it. He was determined not to let anyone, especially his relatives, know what he was up to. He didn't want anyone else's opinions, thoughts or suggestions.

After calmly discussing his decision with Robbin, they both remarkably agreed to a recommendded DIY (Do It Yourself) divorce. They retrieved all their financial records including investments, real estate and retirement accounts. These assets were split evenly down the middle. For cash flow, they agreed that she would receive 30% of the family income for seven years.

Feeling that he had done the right thing for himself and for Robbin, a certain peace settled over him. He could finally exhale.

For her part, Robbin didn't want the inconvenience and embarrassment of a divorce. What would her "clients," her friends think? Would the varnish come off her highly-polished facade? Would she now have to join the unwashed working world? These were the only thoughts that overwhelmed her but at times she felt the need to confide in someone.

During the waiting period, between the filing and the final judgment, trying not to be distracted by negative feelings from the legal issues he was grappling with, Will began giving a lot of his creative energy to an idea he had nourished for quite some time. It had the potential to revolutionize the risk management systems for the insurance, banking and the credit management industries. This technology could possibly save these financial companies hundreds of millions of dollars. Consequently, he could become wealthy beyond his imaginings. Although Will was driven toward success, the thought of money did not move the needle on his happiness meter, not even one tick. He only longed to be free of the burden, the sham his marriage had become.

It was during the mandatory six-month waiting period, over lunch with one of her girlfriends named Carmen, who just happen to work in a local family law office, Robbin confessed her newfound predicament. As she cried out her pain, her sympathetic friend comforted her and suggested that she talk it over with Carmen's boss. Carmen told Robbin, even though Will had made it so that Robbin would not have to worry financially and that there was not another woman involved, he should have to pay for the emotional trauma he was causing her. After all, had he not taken the best years of her life?

Robbin's flaccid mind started working in overdrive.

"Yes." She was being abused, taken advantage of, hurt!

It was now war and she needed a warrior lawyer to help her take Will for all he was worth.

Her new 4'11" attorney literally wrung his hands with anticipation, relishing the idea of getting a hold of Will and his wallet. These were the type of cases this lawyer lived for: abandoned middle age wife being dumped after two decades of dutiful service to a monster of a man who could ultimately pay, pay and pay again.

Robbin's lawyers were elated that they had drawn the soon-to-be-retired Judge Vincent Ulmer to preside over her trial. This judge was known to be sympathetic, if not flirtatiously biased toward women.

The opposite was true for Will and his counsel.

Will should have taken his sister's advice and changed teams as soon as he found out that his case would be tried by a lawyer reputed to be nice and non-aggressive. Will's sister had no fight left in her to convince him, and because of this, the subsequent hard bite he received in the derriere, nicked the bone.

The additional 30% of Will's bonuses and the requirement to pay Robbin's attorneys' fees did not cause Will the most distress. As fate would have it, Robbin's attorneys had intervened a month before the divorce was final. Judge Ulmer, arguably acting way out of his discretion, awarded to Robbin, Will's royalties and licensing agreements for his new process systems as community property, even though it was developed and patented after the date of separation.

"This is outrageous if not illegal," Will vigorously protested to his attorney.

Her lawyer's response was disturbingly dispassionate. She calmly stated, "Any suggestion of judicial bias would be greeted in this court with determined contempt."

Will now knew that he was ruined and this was his "welcome" to Divorce Court 101.

Will could not shake the feeling of abject disillusionment.

What he and Robbin had mutually "agreed" to, lost its first vowel "a" and became fundamentally just "greed."

He constantly kept thinking that he should have dumped her ten years earlier.

Did he really think this would go smoothly? Why did he believe that Robbin would be appreciative of all the things he had done for her and how patient he had been, giving her all the "one more chances" she had begged for?

Something was just not right, how it was all unfolding.

About two years after the Final Disillusionment Of Marriage was mailed to him, Will thought his luck was finally about to change. He heard from a friend that his ex-wife, Robbin, was getting remarried. This meant he would be relieved of future spousal support payments.

He could not have been happier.

It didn't register at first, but when he rifled through his old legal file that was sent to him courtesy of his lawyer, the name popped out like a bolt of lightning. *Ulmer*. Judge Ulmer?

No, it couldn't be.

'There is no way in hell,' he thought.

Just a coincidence, for sure.

A few phone calls and a Google search confirmed all. Robbin was marring the presiding judge in their divorce case and there wasn't a thing he could do about it since the judge had already retired; retired at Will's expense.

A final nail in his fiscal coffin.

~

Three hours later, as Niles and Tiffany finished studying the profiles, it became increasingly and wonderfully clear that this group was not only composed of startling individual stories but the participants themselves represented a dynamic cross section of people devastated by the judicial system.

It had been droned into Tiffany's head over and over again during the laborious hours of her ethics classes, that flammable emotions should be checked at the lab door and that cold, hard, objectivity should remain as the dominate driving force when pursuing scientific understanding. Regardless, her insides were stirring like luscious cream being whipped by a high-speed whisk.

She made a commendable attempted to put on a stoic front that barely masked her unbridled excitement. It was all a performance; she really couldn't wait to get started with the interactive sessions, if only to witness the live (or virtual in this case) drama; the data collection would be a mere bonus.

Tiffany was right.

Niles had painstakingly assembled a remarkable collection of individuals. Any one of them could be the basis of a doctoral case study in its own right. The atmosphere in the room slowly, imperceptibly, changed from acute anticipation to one of reflection...as the core of the human condition came into razor sharp focus.

Niles reread his notes, his thoughts shifted from the primary purpose of the study, the prediction of homicidal precursors, to the potential findings and implications involving the future of relationships in general.

He just could not shake that one burning question: Where was all this headed?

From an evolutionary psychological standpoint, can and how will our species adapt to this increasing level of conflict in relationships?

'What's at stake?' he mused, 'Is the entire concept of long-term pair bonding archaic?'

He shook his head as if to ward off any notion of irrational and alarmist thinking.

'Really,' he thought, 'if traumatic breakups are trending to homicidal thoughts or actions, how do we build the requisite trust so we can love without the fear of bringing harm to ourselves or our partners, especially if our love proves to be misplaced or taken for granted?'

He kept on thinking, 'Studies have shown that more and more people are deciding to live by themselves as opposed to exposing themselves to the potential emotional, psychological and financial risk of coupling.'

The implications were far-reaching.

13

Despite their initial concern about the level of response to the invitations, Niles and Tiffany were very pleased that all the slots for the session had been filled. A total of thirty participants of whom twenty-three were to serve as the control group and seven would participate in the actual session.

To meet the rigorous professional research requirements and adhere to the scientific method, there were two subject selection protocols that had to be met:

(1) Random Selection,
(2) Random Sampling.

This was done with the overall study, however, for the online portion of the study direct selection of the participants was made, based on, court records. As respects to the online portion, it was going to be the first time in history that this type of primary research would be done in the virtual world. The team knew the stakes were going to be high and the peer scrutiny even higher. If the findings were not well documented and/or if it could not be replicated and successfully defended, there could be a lot at risk, both professionally as well as academically.

The participants were provided with state of the art speech recognition software that allowed their avatar to have life-like, real-time communications capabilities. This was important in order to eliminate the lag time customary with typical chat room conversations. Additionally, each subject was given a headset fitted with a neural controller that allowed him or her to manipulate the motor functions of their avatar via – thought and motion waves.

Upon acceptance to participate, each person was furnished with an outline of the project goals along with the requisite disclaimers, disclosures and legal releases. It was with the understanding that this project was part of a scientific study to understand the precursors to personal justice.

What the participants were not ready for, was, the 3D environment which Deuxoverlife.com offered. The chamber was reminiscent of a bygone era of courtrooms like the one would have witnessed in the 16th century at the founding of the first colonies. They were designed to look like the first courthouse/meeting houses in New Haven, Connecticut and had the feeling of the early two story foursquare town halls replete with five bay windows on each side, a steeple and a spire. On the inside were two floors with no walls of separation. Seating was arranged so that all could see one another. Keeping true to history was the old style gallery for women, witnesses and spectators.

This strange juxtaposition of the old colonial with the new and postmodern technology was not lost on any of the attendees.

From a Super Model decked in lingerie, to a Court Jester in colorful costume, sat as jurists in the old limestone and plank wood halls. Seeing this extraordinary contrast rightfully lead the observer to question whether the old rules crafted in our early past, could actually keep up with today's living.

Niles' avatar, appropriately represented as a Basketball Referee, began with a sincere and appreciative welcome to all those in attendance.

"Before we get started, a little background information on the history of our judicial system, I think will help explain, why we are in this setting...and how current laws have evolved to the present day.

"At the time of colonial America, it was common for the accused to sit in a special place in the courtroom called 'the docket.' Witnesses to the crime would be summoned and to personally accuse the suspect. Unless there was refutable testimony, a judge or a panel of judges would pronounce guilt and immediate sentence.

"If you were unfortunate to be accused of a wrong, it was assumed that you were guilty. The modern standard of 'innocent before proven guilty,' was not introduced into the judicial system until several centuries later.

"Because of the expense, the use of personal defense lawyers, even for criminal cases, was extremely rare. All power was vested in the judges, rendering the ability to successfully defend oneself highly unlikely.

"It's true that this procedure was an improvement, but not by much, from ancient barbarism or the medieval process of 'trial by ordeal,' in which the local clergy would look for signs from God as proof of guilt or innocence.

"During Medieval time, under the supervision of a clergyman, an accused person would be put through an ordeal such as having their hands seared with a hot metal poker. If it became infected overnight, that was a sign of guilt from God; if it just blistered, it was a sign of innocence. Alternatively, a suspected person would be dunked in a well or cistern for a time. If they didn't drown, then they were deemed innocent.

"To be sure, we have come a long way in the area of jurisprudence, but given some of the ordeals that people are being put through by the judicial system today, one could argue that we still have a long way to go.

"The initial expeditions and later the colonies, were at first, for-profit corporations that would later become the United States of America. It was no wonder that most lawyers at that time practiced commercial laws of trade. To handle disputes, there were courts that specialized in commercial litigation.

"This kind of legal institution evolved over generations to become the Chancery Court of Delaware. Since most of the lawyers and the courts were focused on commercial law, they applied the same principals they were intimately familiar with to develop the United States Civil Codes...and eventually applied them to the institution of marriage.

"In most states, marriages, including civil unions and common law marriages, are registered and/or governed by the Department of Corporations and when you sign your marriage certificate, you are actually filing incorporation documents and accepting the laws that govern them.

"Effectively, when you get married, you are entering into a business partnership. From the point of view of the state, marriage has nothing to do with love or religion. It's all about business.

"Given that backdrop, we, as they did in former times, are setting up a special court but in this forum we are not going to try commercial disputes, civil litigations or criminal issues. Our special court is going to put justice itself on trial. Instead of having justice try the people, we are going to give the power back to the people and try justice."

A first participant spoke up: "With all due respect, I have had enough with the insides of court rooms. Could I request a change of venue?" Asked, Amazon/Mikki.

A laughter broke out.

"Yes, I'm sure you have," said the vertically-striped Referee, "but I can assure you that this is going to be a different experience than any of you have ever had before."

"How so?" Amazon asked.

"Besides the obviously different modes of communication here in Deuxoverlife.com, you will not be a respondent or a petitioner, but will act as a judge and have a say in the outcome. Moreover, you will be helping advance the discussion regarding the rules we live by."

"So it will be like having a chance to do it all over again? Hmm," considered Amazon.

"Precisely. Are there any other questions or comments before we formally get started?"

"I have a question." announced Court Jester/ Thomas, "You said in the invitation that this was going to be completely anonymous but how do we know for sure that no one here is going to leak who we are in real life?"

"Good question," said Referee Niles, who was thankful that he and Tiffany had spent a great deal of time anticipating these types of questions and much more. "First of all, everyone here has something to lose if there were leaks. Secondly, we will only be identified by our avatars; any real names will not be used. Third- ly, to our knowledge, none of you know each other on a personal or professional level. Fourthly, the sign-on process uses state of the art encryption technology and requires that we all use a remote proxy server that con- tinuously changes its IP address.

"Our security measures have been thoroughly checked to prevent backward tracing. We use a variation of a coded system pioneered by tech gurus Aaron Swartz and Kevin Poulsen called '*DeadDrop*.' Additionally, we are not actually connected to the internet, we are using the Tor Network that has proven to be extremely difficult to monitor by non Tor users.

"Not even the CIA could find out who you are if you carefully follow the instructions that were sent to you."

"I hope you are right," said Court Jester, "I can't afford for any of this to get out."

"We understand." Assured Niles.

"I also have a question," said Faith, hidden behind her peculiar-looking avatar called 'Sheep.' "Do you have any idea how long this is going to take?"

"Each session is designed to last about an hour or so, and we are scheduled to have five sessions over a five week period."

"That's doable," Sheep said. "Thank you."

"If there are no further questions I would like to take this moment to introduce you to my associate, 'The Jock.' The Jock will be taking notes, asking questions and at other times, leading the group.

"Each one of you was selected because you have experienced a significant and traumatic emotional event in your lives regarding trust, relationships and your profound disillusionment with our judicial system in its relationship to marriage, divorce and severing legal ties. These events have exacted a toll from you emotionally, spiritually and financially, with no satisfying resolution in sight. We are here with you to explore the impact all of this has had on you in a non-threatening but openly honest and truthful way...suspending self-censure and judgment.

"It is altogether natural and understandable that when we feel that we've been done horrible wrong, our innate capacity for revenge kicks in and demands justice – especially when we have done everything in our power to be supportive and fair with our partners. When there is an absence of official justice, we tend to create our own."

"Amen!" unexpectedly said Avenging Angel/ Claudia.

"No joke!" Hockey Player/Kyle chimed in.

"So the first topic of discussion is 'fairness.' Do you feel that our judicial system is fair?" The Basketball Referee started with the highly charged question to get things rolling.

"Hell no! It's the furthest thing from fair!" retorted Rock Star/Will

"The system rewards those that contribute the least. And that is the antithesis of fairness." Responded calmly, Super Model/Sumi.

"For example," said Sheep, "my ex-husband not only stole from me, but I have to pay him alimony just because we were married, even though he didn't contribute a penny!"

"I will go you one better," said Rock Star. "My ex refused to work, refused to get an education, even though we didn't have kids. Yet I have to pay her alimony for eleven years just to get rid of her! It's extortion!"

"Why didn't you just kick her to the curb?" snickered Amazon.

"I tried, but I stupidly fell for the old 'give me one more chance' routine that ended up costing me a fortune," said Rock Star.

Court Jester visibly silent, seemed to be focused on a distant point in time.

Avenging Angel said, "The thing that amazes me about relationships is that when you try to be good to others it's taken as a sign of weakness. It identifies you as available for the taking and manipulation by those you care about most. And then when you've had enough and standup for yourself, you're kicked down by a system you were taught that would be just."

"That's your first mistake," sounded almost in a whisper, Court Jester.

"What do you mean by that?" retorted Hockey Player.

"Our justice system, if you can call it that, is not based on whether you are right or wrong or good or bad for that matter; it's about winners and losers. The state requires that everyone only has to understand the number 2." Court Jester explained.

"What the hell does that mean?" asked annoyed, Rock Star.

With an undisguised look of contempt bordering on disgust, Court Jester continued to defend his theory, "Look, in order to simplify, read: dumb-down the divorce process to a one size fits all. The state just uses a formula that even a grade-schooler can understand. Take all the community assets, regardless of individual contribution and divided by 2. And voilá! 'Divorce Made Easy!' But wait! There's more. To lessen the welfare burden on taxpayers, let's wave our magic wand and shift the burden to the higher-earning spouse and by sleight of hand, we have now created wealth without work – the truest definition of welfare. Something that the state despises for itself, has now been sanctioned by the same governing body for the poor sap who's only mistake was to fall in love and just happens to make more money than their spouse!"

"That's the problem," huffed Amazon.

"He's right, if Court Jester is a he...I really can't tell with that getup he or she is wearing," said Sheep. "What I mean is, as my brilliant lawyer made clear to me, we operate in an adversarial Judicial System – so winner takes all."

"Dang!" exclaimed Hockey Player.

"So do you mean we shouldn't be seeking justice from the justice system?" chimed Super Model.

Max Deveraux

"Exactly, your character doesn't count. Divorce is a blood sport – 'Victory over Virtue'" Court Jester stated emphatically.

"Then what the hell are we doing here?" blurted out Rock Star.

"Let me try to answer that one," Jock/Tiffany said, speaking for the first time. "We are here to determine the tipping point of those feeling abused by the legal system; one begins to take matters into their own hands and to seek personal justice as a last resort."

"That's not a difficult task. It's when you're penalized for playing by the rules and then find out that you didn't really know what the rules were." Extolled Amazon.

"She's right. You aren't told the rules until the game is over, and that's not fair," Hockey Player said supportively.

"Look, let's get real," said Rock Star. "We're talking about how the legal system deals with you when a romantic relationship goes south, right? When love turns to hate. I bet I know why they don't fully disclose what you're signing up for. If everyone knew what the rules were going in, no one in their right mind would ever-do it!"

"That is so disparaging, but true. The problem is, there is this huge disconnect between what our assumptions are and what reality is," said Avenging Angel.

Super Model added, "I think Rock Star has a very good point. Just as we've learned that business rules were dictated by lawyers at the founding of this country, so do the rules regarding marriages and civil unions. They're all legislated by politicians and unless you negotiate a prenuptial or cohabitation agreement beforehand, you'll unknowingly accept rules that may not be in your best interest. It's like signing a blank check. And I, in my educated ignorance, have just signed one."

"It all just blows me away," snapped Sheep, "that marriage licenses are held by The Office of the Secretary of State in The Department of Corporations."

"Why should matters of the heart be legislated and then litigated?" Shouted Amazon. "This is wrong on so many levels. That's why people get so pissed and go out for blood at any cost. It can make you so angry you could just kill somebody!"

"First your heart is broken and then your wallet is stolen!" said Hockey Player.

"I thought there was a law against double jeopardy," laughed Avenging Angel.

She was the only one laughing.

"I'm with Amazon on this one," said Court Jester. "I don't necessarily believe that we should all go around taking the law into our own hands but there comes a point when you just want to mess someone up! Hurt them bad, like they hurt you!"

"That's right. Where is O.J. when you need him? That man retired too soon!" said Avenging Angel.

"I hope you don't really mean that," commented Super Model."

"I most certainly do!" responded Avenging Angel.

"Look, I'm no fan of O.J., and I despise what he did, but I can assure you that I understand his anger. Who of us has never thought about taking a deceitful, cold-hearted, ruthless person out?" said Sheep.

The silence in the room reached a crescendo, as each of the participants paused and reflected on Sheep's question.

The reverie was broken by The Referee, "Actually, it is not uncommon for people to have homicidal ideation at one time or another. In fact, in matters of the heart – when people feel betrayed or become victims of adverse justice, desiring the death or even the execution of their duplicitous lovers, comes into their minds more often than you might think. The extreme circumstance is when people act upon their base impulses and commit the murder."

"Wow...before I got here I thought I was the only one who thought about it but was afraid to bring it up for fear of being judged a psychopath," confessed Hockey Player.

"Me too," seconded Super Model.

"Make it three," Amazon agreed with the other two.

"I can't lie, I fight that impulse every day," backed Sheep.

Similar responses came through like falling dominoes.

Jock asked, "If you could get away with the perfect murder of your ex or anyone in which you would never get caught, who here would take steps to make it happen?"

The mostly quiet Court Jester jumped in, "Hell yeah!"

"That's a no-brainer," barked Sheep.

"I'd consider it," said Hockey Player, "but there is no such thing as a perfect murder. I watch '*Forensic Files*,' '*New Detectives*,' all that psycho stuff, and ninety-nine percent of killers get caught over some minute bit of DNA left at the scene."

"I watch '*Snapped on Oxygen*' and sometimes people get away with it and move on with their lives," said Avenging Angel.

"Does getting away with it make it right...just?" asked Jock.

"If we left it up to the legal system, there is no likelihood of rightness or justice either," said Amazon.

"That's true, but it's not always about doing the right thing legally," said Sheep, "sometimes it's about the pure satisfaction of knowing the just thing got done ...and sometimes this may be by any means necessary."

Hockey Player went on a puck-stealing diatribe. "A big part of the problem is that we have too many greedy lawyers that don't give a flying flip about their clients or the opposition. All they care about is getting paid, truth and fairness be damned! They are the ones that have created this mess and they're often the only winners. I mean c'mon, a $199 dollar divorce? They've created a whole new industry, the divorce Industry! This is bullshit! They have no vested interest whatsoever in people resolving their issues in a just manner. They get paid to stoke the already raging fire so they can come in and take your money and claim they saved the day."

Court Jester chimed in, "Okay, I hear you on the lawyer cracks, but let's get back to O.J. for a minute, and this time, personalize it. Let's say that you were in a long-term, horribly abusive and humiliating marriage or relationship – the kind that no one among your family or friends knew about and you just couldn't take it anymore. Then one day, it hit a level that was beyond your capacity to endure or understand and it so happens that you blanked out like Betty Broderick and a gun just unintentionally went off by itself and your spouse just happened to catch a severe case of death. What are you going to do? Throw yourself on the mercy of the court or hope your high-paid lawyer can channel Johnny Cochran and set your guilty-butt free?"

"You sound like a lawyer yourself," said Hockey Player.

It was obvious to Basketball Referee and Jock that things were moving faster than expected.

However, there was an unexpected lull in the heated conversation. The Referee, as if this silence was his cue, called a timeout and declared a break until the following week.

Jock quickly reminded everyone to fill out the online questionnaire.

While a few signed off the session, others took the opportunity to explore different communities of Deuxoverlife.com.

14

When Sumi got offline, she leaned back into her chair, stared out the window and shook her head realizing that she was not the only one harboring a murderous intent. Taking in the events of the last hour, she let out an audible sigh and said, "Wow!"

Unaware her assistant had entered the room, Sumi was startled.

Linda said, "Wow what?"

"Oh...it's nothing."

Linda, had a maternal relationship with her boss, concerned said, "You have every right to be distracted, Honey, given what's been going on with you and that no good cad you're married too."

"Thanks Linda, but I'm fine and by-the-way, it's 'was married.'"

"Of course, and thank God for that!"

"Yes, the divorce may have been finalized but not the residual dishonor or shame," Sumi said as she dazed at the view outside.

Counting the stack of pink pieces of papers on her desk, Sumi was sifting through eight messages. Mixed in between the usual urgent calls from the lab, one captured her attention and curiosity. It was from her brother-in-law, Nolen Roussard, who was married to her younger sister Rebecca.

Sumi was characterized as the compliant one in the family, her beautiful sibling on the other hand was the polar opposite.

Growing up, Rebecca gave their parents fits! Anything they asked her to do, she would do in the exact opposite manner. Never followed the family traditions especially those imported from the old country, Rebecca, the only one in the family born in the States, considered herself more American than Korean.

Sumi loved her sister and she also envied Rebecca's courage to push back against the status quo at times, but it was more – admiration. Sumi constantly acted as the referee between Rebecca and their parents, especially with her father. She was especially struck by her sister's unwavering defiance when it came to personal choices. Rebecca literally exhausted her mother and father.

However, there was one area that Rebecca did comply with her elders' wishes; in marring Nolen, at least she did not bring home a Japanese man.

If relishing in every opportunity to shock her parents, Rebecca married Nolen Roussard, an African-American. He qualified as her Coup de Grâce.

It wasn't that Rebecca married Nolen because he was black or that it would provoke her parents...that was just an added bonus. But that Nolen was a good catch by any measure. He was drop-dead gorgeous and the type who promised beautiful children. He was highly educated, with a master's degree in criminal science and although not a practicing attorney, he earned a JD from Loyola Law School.

Nolen was rumored to be on the short list of future candidates for Chief of Police for the City of Los Angeles.

His fame in local and nation-wide law enforcement came about when he was a member of his union's political action committee. As a board member, he pushed to have all guns sold in the United Sates, whether imported or domestic, be fired so that shell casings could be collected prior to sale creating a bullet database. This was similar to AFIS (Automated Fingerprint Identification System) and would allow, as Nolen preached, the ability to set up a database that would connect all bullets with firearms. This database would allow police to locate the original owners. He claimed that this would certainly expedite solving crimes.

Nolen caught hell from the NRA and their political allies but he stood his ground and was hailed as a role model by peace officers and the country as a whole admired his courage.

Rebe, as Sumi called her, had done well, yet stayed true to herself; getting her daughterly jabs in. Rebecca's shortened name would often make Sumi smile; it truly suited her sister's rebellious personality.

Because Sumi would rarely hear directly from Nolen, she became concerned that her sister or her family be in some sort of trouble.

Sumi dropped the other message slips and immediately dialed Nolen's number.

"Federal Bureau of Investigation, Los Angeles SAC (Special Agent in Charge) Office," efficiently announced the operator.

"Agent Roussard, please."

"Whom should I tell Special Agent Roussard, is calling?"

"It's Sumi Kim, his sister-in-law."

"Thank you."

A few moments later, Nolen came on the line. "Hi Sumi. Thanks for getting back to me."

"Nolen. Is everything okay? Rebe and the kids...?" Sumi asked nervously.

"Yes. Rebe and the children are fine."

"Oh, that's a relief. You had me a little frightened there for a minute. I don't recall you ever calling me at work."

"True, but that is exactly why I'm calling. It is about work."

"Go on."

"When you were over for dinner Sunday, I couldn't help but overhear part of the conversation you had with Rebe about the new program you're developing. I think you called it DEP or something."

"ADEP. That's short for Advanced DNA Extrapolation Program."

"Yeah, that's it. I only heard a little bit but I was intrigued nevertheless. I was wondering if you wouldn't mind telling me a little more about it. I'm always interested in any furtherance in forensic science that can better facilitate our investigations. Even though we've come a long way, it seems that perps are always inventing new and creative ways not to get caught."

"Well, I think we may be getting a little ahead of ourselves here. We haven't even begun the beta test."

"Beta test...?"

"I mean we don't yet know if it's going to work."

"So it's just a working theory then?"

"Well, I would like to think we're past the theoretical stage, but yes, it hasn't been proven outside the lab."

"Can you tell me about it anyway?"

"Sure, but I must warn you, you're going to have to go back to your classroom days and put on your biology and statistics hats."

"I was afraid of that."

Sumi explained the ADEP program took DNA identification to the next logical level: that of visual identification. That she assigned numerical values to all the possible genetic markers found on the alleles of the chromosomes. These alleles recognized hair color, eye color, ears size, shape and length of the nose, how the earlobe was attached or detached to the head, whether a person would have straight or kinky hair, or premature baldness. What gender or race a person was, and the size, shape, and width of their mouth and lips. Whether he or she would have freckles or in need of corrective lenses. What the color and tone of the skin would be. What all the combinations of features a specific individual person would have – the list went on.

"The alleles dictate even the slight nuanced variations in identical twins," Sumi went on, "even though they share the same DNA."

She explained that recent advancements in scientific understanding of genetics have helped to identify certain markers in the genetic code that would have been considered science fiction just a few years ago.

"After ADEP program assigns digital or numerical values to each of the possible characteristics found on the alleles it then runs what is called multivariate probability analysis of random possibilities. Next, based on certain algorithmic parameters, it predicts the highest and most likely combinations of facial features and then uses image technology to paint a high -resolution 3D digital picture of the result on a computer screen."

"That is mind boggling!" said Nolen. "To be honest, I didn't understand all of it, but it sounds a bit like what they do when they age-progressed pictures for abducted children on the backs of milk cartons."

Laughing, Sumi said, "A rather crude analogy, but yes, that's the idea."

"If what you're up to, works, Sumi, it will put a lot of forensic artists out of business!"

"Not at all. I believe our technology will assist in the process of developing investigative cases, insofar as forensic artists, they work with witnesses and ADEP will not. As you well know, it's common practice for forensic anthropologists and sculptors to use established knowledge about the relationships between body measurements and construction and facial characteristics to help establish identity when you don't have a complete set of bones or only a skull without a face or skin to work with.

"For example, if you have only a femur bone you can accurately predict height, arm span, weight, as well as gender. And the triangular distance between eye sockets and mouth is a constant. Also, the skin depth on the face of each of us is typically determined by bone structure.

"All these known qualities and relationships are written in code on our DNA at conception. Our DNA gives instructions imbedded in our cells, chromosomes and alleles. ADEP takes all this to the next level and rebuilds a virtual 'us' based on a digital representation of that code." Explained Sumi.

"I can tell you this for sure, Sumi, if ADEP works, its applications to law enforcement worldwide are infinite."

"Actually, I have had the same thought."

"So where are you in the process?"

"I'm just about to run my first trial run," said Sumi.

"Listen, I know the courts are very careful about accepting new and unproven science into evidence, however there are breakthroughs. And since we are not running out of criminals anytime soon, I would be more than happy to assist you in any way I can. I'm sure there will be a suitable test case we can work together on."

"Thank you, Nolen for your interest and support, but as of right now I'm afraid we are not yet ready for primetime. However, should the beta test work, I just might be knocking on your door."

"Or I, yours."

"That works for me. By the way, Nolen, how severe are the penalties for cyber-trespassing?"

"It depends. Why?"

"Just curious."

"Which killed the cat," laughed Nolen.

15

After the first session was over, Niles and Tiffany took some time to debrief and begin documenting their findings. They were both extremely pleased that overall, it went very smoothly, although somewhat taken aback by the depth of hostility generated by the group. It wasn't that the spectrum of negative feelings weren't expected but just to see it in person or virtually in person was truly fascinating.

They speculated about the acceptance the online community platform would receive from their peers. It was unusual but no one could argue successfully against its effectiveness. Its novelty notwithstanding, Niles and Tiffany were now certain that the candor of the discussion was due to the anonymity factor provided by Deuxoverlife.com.

Niles commented on the possibility that once their paper was published and the acceptance of Deuxoverlife.com was gained, there might be a shift in how therapy, especially on the group level, would be conducted. By using the online virtual world, the stigma of counseling would continue to erode. After all, no one would have to sneak around and look over their shoulder when going to see their therapist. The ultimate in privacy could be achieved.

Niles continued to muse over the seemingly unlimited application of Deuxoverlife.com. Particularly he felt there was a possible medical use for doctors and their patients. They could benefit from the program's utility in communicating confidential medical information such as STD transmission and treatment.

Once they finished writing the preliminary overview of the first session, they discussed possible changes to the direction of the next session. They wondered if there should be more control or guidance of the conversation or allow it to continue as user-directed.

They chose the latter.

They discussed their relative findings and what relationship it had, if any, on the predictions of their model.

The conversation turned to the research protocols: Tiffany's preliminary findings from the data inputs and running the Step Wise Regression (correlation analysis) and ANOVA (analysis of variance) between groups.

"Okay Tiffany, before you explain your findings, humor me by restating the project's Null Hypothesis, giving its definition and providing an example. I know you know all this, but I want to use this opportunity to prep you for the part of the oral exam of your thesis."

"No Problem. The Null Hypothesis or unacceptable conclusion is: H0 = Adverse Judgment is not linked to Spousalcide. On the other hand, H1 = Adverse Judgment is a precursors to Spousalcide.

"In scientific and statistical analysis, the Null Hypothesis is the opposite of your hypothesis. In other words, you're trying not to prove something but trying to disprove that your idea is correct, thereby rejecting the Null Hypothesis.

"An example: Let's say you are trying to determine whether pornography is a cause of rape. You don't try to prove that rape and pornography are correlated; your goal is to try and prove that they are unrelated. If you can't disprove that, then it becomes self-evident that they are related.

"And by the way, there have been actual studies that prove that the two are not related and that peeping-tom-ism and burglary are better at explaining non-date rape."

"Excellent!" said Niles. "I can see that you're catching on quick! Now let's get back to what you wanted to show me regarding your findings."

"Sure, Dr. Niles. This first chart shows that in the last five years in California, there were a total of 6,758 cases of reported spousalcide. Of these, there were 3,726 cases that were adjudicated by the courts. These included child custody disputes, but the majority were property settlement cases.

"Of these cases, when there was a significant difference in earning capacity between the couples, with one spouse having to provide the majority of the other spouse's support, after the divorce, there was a disproportionate increase in the murder rates."

"That seems to support the expectations," said Niles, "but did you uncover any relationship to longevity in marriages with spousalcide outcomes?"

"Good question," said Tiffany, "and yes, I did. As we have previously discussed, in California as well as in other community property based states, the rule of thumb is that the higher-earning spouse pays 40% of their gross income less 50% of the lower-earning spouse's actual wages for half the length of the marriage for up to about ten years. Anything over ten years remains with the jurisdiction of the court; which means that the higher-earning spouse could conceivably pay their ex for the rest of their life. This is similar to but not as extreme as the lifetime support states such as Massachusetts, New Jersey and Florida

"The relevance of these facts to our study is that when you look at this next chart you will see the rate of spousalcide dramatically spikes upward at approximately seven years and begins to accelerate as the duration of the relationship increases. In other words, the longer the marriage lasts, the higher the chances of murder at the hands of the paying spouse.

"As alarming as this is, it can be understood in light of the incentives for murder. The longer the duration of the marriage, the longer the higher-earning spouse has to pay."

"That's cold-blooded," stated Niles, then asked, "Are you suggesting that the data shows that it's all about the money?"

"I'm not trying to lock myself in, Dr. Niles, to any particular inference at this point, but it does seem, at least from a directional standpoint that either money or some sub-factor such as shouldering the economic burden for the majority of the time during their marriage are both likely factors. When the higher-earning spouse is ordered to continue paying with no end in sight, they may use murder in the same way an actuarial does, by redlining insurance applicants when trying to limit their downside risk."

"I applaud you for guarding your biases and maintaining your scientific skepticism at this juncture, Tiffany; however, as I see the numerical results here in the output sheets and histogram distributions, correlation indicators of .08 are very strong indeed! And it looks like there's not much wiggle room for any other conclusions. But let's table that discussion for later." Niles still looking at the output sheets, continued. "I'm curious. What have you found regarding the relationships between growth in the legal industry and the length of time in granting final dissolution?"

"That one was really an eye opener! Refer to this table for the raw data and then look at how this other chart here shows the cross correlations. After a significant drop in the time it takes for a divorce to become final, there has been a recent upward trend in the length of disputes. Although this increase is measured in months, its financial impact is very significant.

"Additionally, and as can be expected, there has been a steady increase in graduating law students choosing family law as a specialty. Moreover, there has been a rise in major law firms adding family practice to their service menus.

"These trends could be explained by the dramatic increase in divorce rates but that doesn't give the complete picture. When I interviewed people at several influential bar associations, I was quite astonished by some of their comments.

"One woman told me that when this state changed to a no-fault status, it was designed to make the courts more efficient and expedite the process. It worked for a while because the need for extensive discovery was diminished due to not having to prove such things as infidelity and other character flaws.

"At the same time, the legislature adopted and put into law new guidelines administering the division of assets, especially the ones for spousal support. Incidentally, that's when the name changed from 'alimony,' which is derived from the Latin word for 'aliment,' meaning sustenance or nourishment; to 'spousal support,' which is ironic since it should arguably be called 'ex-spousal support.' That's just my opinion.

"But one of the unintended consequences of this action is that it opened the door to abuse, both in terms of the legal counsel and the contestants themselves. 'Clever attorneys' saw an opportunity to recapture billable hours lost due to judicial efficiency by creating artificial demands such as battling for long-term support while suppressing their recipient clients' ability to be gainfully employed and self-supporting." Tiffany flipped through the report looking for a specific page, then continued, "Not to be overlooked as a revenue stream by the cottage industry of single practice family law attorneys: the invention of the pedestrian version of the pre-nuptial agreement that had previously been reserved for nobles.

"There is also evidence that when attorneys, through their bar associations were allowed to advertise, there was a sudden jump in the number of divorces. This also had an impact of the longevity of marriages. And why not? At a bargain 'come on' price of $199.00 what tortured soul could resist? Everyone that has ever taken an introductory economics course knows that when prices fall demand goes up!

"As far as trends are concerned, despite many attempts to stop the rise in divorce rates, the climb continues unabated. The only exception being that during economic recessions, the financial cost of divorce outweighs the expected relief of pain and suffering by staying married. Rates of divorce slow during times when disposable income shrinks or there is economic uncertainty."

"That seems rather bleak," said Niles.

"True," said Tiffany, "but another sociological inference can be possibly gleamed from this: it may be that couples faced with serious economic issues as a proxy for survival are more likely to pool resources and focus their collective energy on outside threats to happiness instead of internal ones."

"Makes sense to me. After all, survival is our primary instinct from an evolutionary standpoint."

"That's what I have been taught...by you, Dr. Niles."

"Brilliant work, Tiffany...just brilliant!"

"Thank you."

"So I have been promoted?" to Niles, "Have I?"

"Let's just say you should never underestimate the motivating power of non-solicitous praise, plus you have earned it."

Max Deveraux

16

When Sumi met Zeke at their scheduled Thursday night meeting, Zeke was pleasantly surprised that she had chosen to be a subject for the beta testing of ADEP.

Zeke expressed some trepidation when Sumi resisted disclosing the identity of the test subject. She was protecting the integrity of the experiment and at the same time she didn't want to get into a debate about her choice.

Sumi's choice was not unheard of in the annals of scientific history. In many experiments, especially ones that had to do with biological discoveries, scientists would routinely try new methods on themselves first. At times this resulted in new discoveries that would benefit mankind but sometimes would end in miserable deaths.

Sumi knew however, that using herself might not pass the muster of peer review. Before she could submit her discovery to *Scientific Monthly, Popular Science* or any of the top-level industry publications, she would have to somehow give the impression that her first would be an independent subject. This was imperative because of the possibility of her being accused of scientific fraud, especially given some of the recent and tragically embarrassing high profile cases of scientists taking shortcuts by doctoring results or publishing their findings prematurely.

Sumi would not take the chance that someone could claim contamination with the results at best and biased manipulation at worst.

The real issue gnawing at her was not the selection of a suitable subject. She knew she could take up her brother-in-law Nolen's offer to help solve a live case. Her primary concern was in the stealing of computing power. What was beyond her comprehension was that her participation in one of the greatest leaps forward in our use of DNA could, as a reward, land her in jail! But most of all having to explain this to her father and mother.

This was no mere fabrication fueled by paranoia on her part. Sumi knew that in order for ADEP to be accepted by the scientific community, it would have to be able to independently replicate the results. The nagging question was: where would *they* get the computing power?

As it was, no matter what Zeke or anyone else said to allay her fears, in truth, she felt like a thief. What they were doing made the hackers involving Chinese cyber-espionage look like boy scouts. It bothered her immensely! The more she thought about it, her hatred for those "Nuns" increased.

Her only redeeming thought that ameliorated the situation was: "If it all works as planned, perhaps NSA might intervene and provide entry to the Lawrence Livermore Labs Sequoia computer."

Sumi knew she could not cower now. She had to push on, come what may.

Exasperated, she wondered, 'Where is David Hume, the father of modern ethics, when you needed him?'

Moving past her own *Private Idaho*, she committed to handing over to Zeke the slides containing her DNA sequence. Her essence. Herself.

This was no longer just business. It was very, very personal. It put new meaning to the phrase "put your soul in it."

She was all in.

She didn't merely invent ADEP.

She was ADEP!

A few days prior meeting Zeke, Sumi began the first part of the two-stage process. First she wiped the inside of her mouth with a cotton swab. Done to obtain a sample of DNA from her epithelial cells. This DNA would later be dissolved in a benign solvent so that all other materials would be separated and the DNA base of ATCG, (Adenine, Thymine, Cytosine, and Guanine) would be isolated. Then she ran a process of PCR (Polymerase Chain Reaction) to replicate the DNA strands so she would have enough of a sample to test.

She thought, 'Fortunately, each DNA molecule contains a complete set of our entire genetic make-up. What makes us unique is the order of our individual alphabet. The sequence in one person could be GCTA …and in another it could be TACG…for the same chromosomes; however the combination "TA" and the combination "CG" remain the same. Sampling and extracting DNA is not as sexy as what is shown on the popular prime time television shows as such as *CSI*.'

Sumi knew that every step of the process had to be painstakingly executed to produce uncontaminated results.

She marveled at the beauty of the double helix design of the DNA molecular structure as she viewed it through her electron microscope. Peering into the basic building blocks of genetic make-up, she could not help but recall how the discoverers themselves described what they first saw in 1951:

"...This (DNA) structure has two helical chains each coiled round the same axis...Both chains follow right handed helices...the two chains run in opposite directions...The bases are on the inside of the helix and the phosphates on the outside..."

These phosphate bases of GATC were the key to the whole puzzle, which Sumi was working hard at unlocking. There were over three billion base pairs of GATC in each individual genomes, the sequencing would have been daunting for her, were it not for the HGP or Human Genome Project and the vast library of information made public.

The permutations or order of repetitive appearances of each of the separate substances determined what characteristics would be found on the alleles of the chromosomes. Since there could literally be trillions of permutations, ADEP's job was to, first, detect and analyze the string of patterns, next, run millions of simulations of possible results, then, predict and select the most probable or optimum outcome, and finally, render a digital facial representation.

The most powerful of all ADEP's capabilities was its age progression or AP feature. The AP part of the program allowed a user to use a sliding scale tab at the bottom of the frame similar to a volume control on a Digital Video Recorder. This would allow the user to see what a person, barring injury and/or plastic surgery, would look like during the various stages of life.

Although ADEP's inherited capabilities ranging from conception forward, given billions of cellular divisions and additional computing power it would consume, Sumi and Zeke isolated the output range from 40 to 80 years of age. The decision was made due, in large part, because of its predicted initial use; such as kidnappings, missing persons, archeology and law enforcement.

Despite Sumi remaining unsure, she was amused by Zeke's seemingly nutty idea of a marriage application for ADEP. Stranger things had happened such as the current use of the botulism toxin Clostridium Botulinum, commonly known by its commercial name, BOTOX.

Injecting food poison into your one's face must have also sounded crazy at the beginning but now many women (and increasingly men), were using it with such ardent zeal, it would even make Dorian Grey blush!

After Sumi applied the four colored dyes, which attach to corresponding protein bases of GATC, was ready to run the sample through the special detector that would identify each of the pairs and their respective orders. As the detector identified each color, it applied the corresponding alphabetic letters of T, C, G, or A, and assigned each a numerical value, then simultaneously entered the letters with their corresponding digits in the designated database.

Sumi copied the code on to the portable "Le Cie" hard-drive and delivered it to Zeke.

The entire process took four days.

Sumi confidently had followed the preliminary steps to the letter, however, the magnitude of what she was attempting, made her otherwise, calm self, - very anxious.

She could hardly stand the wait until her theory was confirmed.

17

A week later, as Sumi was driving on her way to finally deliver the data set to Zeke, she bombarded herself with random thoughts. Her own DNA sequence sitting in the passenger seat in the bowls of a thumb-drive made her think as if she was transporting her own urn of ashes. The dominant thought that consumed her, however was her reflecting on the first Deuxoverlife.com session. It had become an obsession.

Oddly, she did not focus on anything in particular; it was the entire experience that she could not shake.

Expressing her persona through her avatar was fascinating. To be able, to dress and say whatever she wanted without reprisal or judgment for the first time was intoxicating.

"Why couldn't the real world be like that?" she wondered out loud.

Spending her whole life trying to please others and living up to their expectations while suppressing her own desires had made Sumi ill. Especially allowing people like Brad to presume upon her. When she was online at Deuxoverlife.com, she felt free to express herself openly, without the fear of rejection. She couldn't wait to log-on once again.

'Good thing for GPS,' Sumi thought as she pulled up to what seemed to be an abandoned building. For the life of her, she couldn't understand why Zeke lived in such a horrible neighborhood, right in the heart of the skid row district. She knew it wasn't due to his finances; because Zeke, for all his quirkiness, had done exceptionally well as a "hired-gun" to fix nasty computer glitches. And for several highflying Internet start-ups, he had made billionaires out of people like himself and his geeky "coder" friends. She surmised wealth did not necessarily guarantee good sense or security.

Sumi pushed the amber colored button, on the left side of the front door, next to a box that housed a keypad.

"Who is it?" Zeke's voice crackled through the speaker.

"It's me, Sumi."

"Sure, put in the passcode I'll gave you." Zeke whispered.

"What's up with all the James Bond stuff? I did not know I was entering the bottom floor of NORAD!" Sumi said quizzically.

"You can never be too careful. Were you followed?" Zeke asked cautiously.

"Are you kidding me? You think I'm going to be looking over my shoulder just to come to this dump?" Sumi said with a tinge of sarcasm.

"It may look like a dump to you, but as far as security goes, it doesn't get any better than this."

"My bad, I must have mistaken that guy who's passed out in the gutter out here for a bum. I take it he's really head of your security detail?" Sumi laughed.

"You're real funny Sumi, that's not the kind of security I'm talking about and you know it. This is the last place a spook is going to look for an international power thief."

"Well, I'm glad you cleared that up Sherlock. I was beginning to think I'd misjudged the poor guy. Seriously, what about my car Zeke? I hope I don't find it up on cinderblocks when I get back."

"Look, it's not like anyone is rolling around here with a tire iron, jacks and some blocks. As long as you don't have any cigarettes, weed or a forty in plain sight, you should be cool. Don't get so hung up. It's just metal anyway." Zeke assured her.

As Sumi put in the passcode, she couldn't help but wonder what she'd gotten herself into.

As soon as the buzzer sounded, she went inside the ramshackle building. It was clear that Zeke didn't put a high premium on a room-with-a-view. Instead of going up a flight of stairs or taking an elevator to a top floor, the only opening led down to a basement. The large set of double doors one finds in a meat locker were unlocked, Sumi entered Zeke's living quarters.

The place looked nothing like what she had expected. It was tastefully decorated; a huge room sectioned off in various areas according to obvious uses.

There was an industrial feel to the space with high-tech retro vibe. It reminded her of an upper floor of a loft with at least twenty feet high ceilings. At the corner was a large gourmet kitchen area equipped with the latest stainless steel appliances.

The living room, the center from where everything radiated, was decked-out in high-grade fabrics and leather sofas, and accented with oversized end-tables. The cubist-style art pieces were immense and leaned toward unabashed hints of Picasso-esque influences.

Except for the absence of natural light, Sumi was truly impressed. It was not how she thought a hermit like Zeke, would be living.

"Wow your place is…" Sumi said but was unable to find the right words.

"You thought I lived in a cave, huh?"

"Let's just say it doesn't match certain aspects of your personality." Sumi quickly shot back.

"You think you know someone. We can only conclude that there are many dimensions of me, which I have never been given the chance to reveal to you." Continued Zeke.

"I think we've already had that discussion, and as you well know, I'm married." Sumi reminded him.

"Were married." Quipped Zeke.

"What?" Sumi said not completely understanding Zeke's words.

"I said you were married, past tense." Zeke said with emphasis.

"I did not come here to discuss my current status." Sumi said in a very guarded manner.

"I know that, but you may consider using some of that infinite brain power of yours to come to your senses and see what's in front of you." He said with a mischievous smile.

"If I do and that is one big if, I'll let you know, but in the mean time we have a ton of work to do and the sooner we get started, the better." Sumi said without looking directly at him.

"You can't rush these things. This type of programming requires a lot of patience." Zeke reminded Sumi.

"That may be true to a point, but this idea of ADEP has been floating out there ever since I applied for the temporary patent and as many brilliant scientist that worked on the Genome Project with us, someone is bound to be tinkering around with a similar application. I don't want to be caught flat-footed, basking in naive bliss." Sumi responded.

"Point taken. Do you have the sample?" He asked.

"Right here." Sumi said as she waived the small envelope in Zeke's direction.

"Cool. Let's go to the boiler room." Zeke said as he pointed his hand in a leading gesture.

Zeke led Sumi to an adjacent anteroom with its own set of double doors, which opened to an 8x10 space. This led to another set of thick metal double-doors with massive hinges that reminded her of the entrance to a bank vault.

Zeke's over-the-top entry sequence to go into the chamber included a retinal scan, voice analysis, a full hand match and something she had never seen or heard of: a lip impression. It all seemed to Sumi like a ritual reserved for a members-only entrance to an "*Eyes Wide Shut*" secret sex society.

She just shook her head without comment and kept moving.

Finally, they entered the chamber. Sumi wasn't sure what to expect, what she saw was far outside any of her imaginings. It was a boiler room conceived by a madman! It had a row of six huge, very comic-book-like old boilers.

'Thank God they aren't functioning. It'd be hot as hell in here if they were,' she thought.

What she saw next threw her equilibrium off almost to the point of disorientation. What lay before her, justified all the crazy security that Zack had contrived.

In the middle of the room was a plain table with a huge see through glass monitor. The monitor was the largest she had ever seen and she had seen plenty.

On top of the table was one huge nine cubic feet transparent Plexiglas square box all lit up inside. She did not understand it. She thought there should have been at least a minimum of a few large servers – a cluster of small machines connected to all kinds of gadgets and gizmos.

'But, my God, the room is practically empty!' she thought.

Sensing the apparent shock on Sumi's face, Zeke walked over to the table and said, "Sumi, meet Slave Driver, Slave Driver say 'hi' to Sumi."

A disembodied but not unfriendly androgynous voice said in a very clear tone, "Hello, Sumi, Zeke has told me a lot about you. He likes you, you know."

To this Zeke quickly said, "That was a private conversation, SD, remind me not to confide in you."

Sumi, not understanding the social graces required at the moment, said, "Hi."

"I bet you were expecting some type of command center like what you have seen at the movies in those over-hyped, high-budget, substance-lacking films, huh?" Zeke asked.

"Something like that, yes."

"That's so old school, so old world. Our world is not about owning information but having access to information; that's the real power. Most of the information-rich countries and companies don't have a clue how to use the information they have. To them, data mining is just a cliché. They don't even know how to construct the right questions to get the most potent answers.

"There is so much information out there, that there is a cure for every disease ever known to man right at their fingertips...if only they knew what to ask! An even greater crime is that the answers to all geopolitical and social challenges are obtainable, if only the right questions were asked. But most of the information is held in private hands and therefore rendered useless because of inane territorial issues and gratuitous greed. If all the stockpile of information held on PCs and other servers around the globe were linked, it would be the most powerful resource ever invented by man. I will stop preaching: What man has failed to do, SD will do." Said Zeke.

"Thank you Zeke, that's the best compliment I have ever received. I didn't know you cared so much," commented Slave Driver.

"You're welcome, SD, and by the way, Sumi, by not storing all the data here – helps security. No one will be able to trace our searches back to this location. Also, it removes the issue of theft. At least how I define theft."

"I don't know what to say"

"No words needed, just give me the thumb drive." Zeke plugged the portable drive into SD's USB port and then they both watched, as the machine performed a preliminary virus and content scan of the information at lightning speed and completed multiple error checks to determine the completeness of the data set.

Minutes later, when SD was finished, its voice said, "Ready to Roll."

"Is SD your alter-ego or are you related? You two sound alike." Sumi said jokingly.

"Let's just say, SD did get a life, when I registered on Ancestry.com." Zeke chuckled.

"Thought so." Sumi said directing her reply to no one in particular.

"So who is the subject?" asked Zeke.

"I thought you might ask, but for now let's just keep it anonymous. That way, we'll be assured that the integrity of the process is not compromised." Sumi said nodding her head in an assuring manner.

"No sweat!" Zeke said sensing there was no point in pushing the issue.

"Can you enlighten me on the next steps of the process and what to expect as far as procedures and timeline?" asked Sumi.

"Sure, of course. I have already preloaded the ADEP program and now that Slave Driver has the raw digitized DNA sequence, along with the specific allele markers of all twenty-three chromosomes, it's ready to do its thing. That is to say, the first step is to search the

Internet and identify available supercomputers that are currently not being used at full capacity.

"We will pass on any system that is running at more than 65% and will not use more than 1% of any one server. This is a necessary precaution against tripping system monitors as well as avoiding trigger capacity overloads. Once the megaservers have been identified, we will begin the process of linking them together in groups or teams using a daisy chain model that rolls from one server to another. We will then assign each team of computers a specific task based on ADEP's ordinal protocols.

"Next, each subgroup will run multiple probability analyses on its section of the project and will check in to see if its conclusions are congruent with the master controller. This step is important to maintain a dependable level of output to make sure that no rogue group happens upon an anomaly and believes that it is representative of the rest of the team's findings.

"For example, there are obvious genetic markers that determine sex, ethnic group, probable height, weight set-point, hair color, etc., but within these characteristics there is a lot of variance. We do not want one team to assume, in a vacuum, that because there is a 99.8% probability that a person of African-American descent will have black hair, when another group finds that the probability is actually 99.899% that the hair is black with a slight auburn tint.

"The rule is that the higher the probability, the greater the certainty. The final call will be made by the master controller. Since there are literally trillions of possibilities, it's important to have a default mechanism in place or we may end up recreating a platypus or even worse, a Frankenstein." Zeke explained.

"Yes, that would be a disaster." Sumi agreed.

"Once the numbers have been crunched and the override decisions have been made, SD will begin to build a line-by-line 3D model of the results. Since we have created ADEP with the ability to isolate specific sections of the body, we will run this test on everything from the neck up. Thank God you thought of this, as interesting as it might be visually, it would take us forever if we had to run it on the entire Human-Andros." Zeke continued.

"What are the risks?" Sumi asked.

"I'm sure there will be a lot of issues that will come up that we have not considered but for the most part, ADEP is based on very sound science. The only thing I am concerned about now is the calibration. No doubt there will be some tweaking that will have to be done as we go forward until we get things within an acceptable range but I have a high degree of confidence that we are on the right track."

"So when are we going to begin?" Sumi asked with a look of sheer anticipation.

"Because we are dealing with literally every time-zone in the world, SD has estimated that the optimal time when we will have the most idle computing capacity is between 24:57 and 26:18 hundred hours GMT or more precisely, 4:57 AM and 6:18 AM our time. This will change each day as we run additional lines of code." Zeke said with confidence.

"Well Zeke, I must say, I'm impressed!"

"I'm glad you like." Zeke said proudly.

"It feels like we are waiting for election results from different precincts around the country." Sumi mused.

"That's an excellent analogy." Zeke replied nodding his head.

"I take it, you're going to call me, as results come in?" Sumi said looking for assurance.

"You bet your sweet...you know what I mean." Zeke caught himself in mid-sentence.

"That's what I'm afraid of." Sumi said, anticipating the typical male response.

Sumi needed to get back to her office to prepare for the next Deuxoverlife.com session, so she declined Zeke's offer for tea, even though he had made a special effort to get her favorite, which could only be ordered online at Heavenlytea.com.

For Sumi, it was hard not to stay. What made it even more difficult was that she was craving the attention only males could provide. But in regards to Zeke, despite his idiosyncratic ways, was so amazingly interesting to talk too. It also didn't help that seeing him in his environment for the first time made him seem less strange and somewhat even attractive in an unexpected sort of way. However, as Sumi considered her current circumstances, she put such implausible thoughts out of her mind. After a few moments, she said goodbye and left.

As she stepped outside Zeke's building, a wave of relief swept over her when she saw that her 2013 Audi A6 was right where she had left it and not hoisted on cinderblocks!

18

With murderous intensity, the hacker furiously worked the numeric keyboard of the computer. He applied his highly developed math skills to the task of using remote network servers to mask his identity. His mind occupied with his own personal mission of direct justice. To his twisted way of thinking, his other heinous acts were easy; compared to this one. This was his boldest step so far. Once the process had begun there would be no turning back, no excuses.

What had to be done, had to be done.

It was not about compassion for any particular poor sap. Some of them were deserving of what their stupidity and ignorance had wrought. This was for the sake of the system – a system that was severely broken and in need of emergency triage. The implications were as far reaching as the necessary remedies were bold.

The killer reasoned, the irony of it all was that the methods used to get to this point were not of any use to get out of the quagmire.

It appeared that the issue had escaped the notice of the victims – as if a collective agreement to suffer in silence and isolation had been signed.

In the past, when groups of Americans were the targets of judicial bias and they felt disenfranchised, they'd band together to protest, challenge and ultimately bring a change to the system. American history has been replete with examples of these momentous revolutionary transformations. But for unknown reasons, on this issue, despite the obvious fact, the pendulum had swung too far in a disturbingly discriminating direction. People were not collectively protesting at all but inevitably, as individuals, were compelled to take the law into their own hands.

The cases should have been instructive but instead had only been used to entertain the prurient voyeurs. The Hacker felt that America had developed an untreatable strain of impotence – an emasculation of will.

But unless there was a consequence for not changing, there was no motivation to fight the inertia. There would have to be a price to pay and a sacrifice to be made.

A message had to be conveyed.

A wakeup call had to be announced. And he had the number.

~

The two previous trial runs came off without a hitch. Now, it was show time. Remarkable as it was, the passcode for the VPN (Virtual Private Network,) had not been changed. It was amazing to him how careless people were when caught up in the euphoria, which comes when getting something one does not earn. The Hacker mused that a person didn't have to look far for examples of this; just look at lottery winners! Half of them went bankrupt within a few years of winning. The old adage: "Nothing earned, nothing gained," (and: "Nothing remained"), still had its merits.

This VPN app was the latest on the market and the whole system was estimated to have cost the hapless original owner of this so-called "Smart Home," over $500,000.

It was worth it.

Not only did it allow Internet access to all the cameras in and outside the house, it made available remote control of nearly all functions that could be actuated by its electronic brain.

A person could remotely turn on any one of the thirty-two flat screen televisions in addition to the two-story, two-screen private theater – any one of which could be reversed and used as a surreptitious camera. One could turn on and set the temperature to all eight baths and showers, as well as the pool, spa, fire-pit and fireplaces.

One could even have their favorite Chardonnay chilled to the perfect temperature, waiting for one's arrival. The heating and lighting systems were key-strokes away. The doors and locks were at one's finger-tips. This was all a huge advancement in convenience for deliveries, maintenance, comfort and security.

Perfect for The Hacker's purposes as well.

He had studied his target well.

Anika was consistent if nothing else.

The Hacker had Anika's routine down to the minute.

Every Monday, Wednesday and Friday, after she spent three rigorous hours working out with her trainer in her private gym, she spent the next thirty minutes in the steam room in her downstairs spa until Sven, her Nordic masseuse, would arrive at 11:30 A.M. The only variation in Anika's weekly routine was that on Friday, after Sven left, she got back in the steam room for a twenty-minute spiritual release using aromatherapy and meditation.

As she lay on the imported leather massage table overlooking the backyard patio and pool, the pleasure in her eyes was undeniable.

The view from there was nothing less than spectacular! The greenest of green grass of the eleventh fairway of Southern-Highlands Private Golf course provided an astounding contrast to the parched desert terrain of Nevada. In the far distance, the skyline of the "Strip" rose from the dust as if claiming the birthright of Phoenix from its sibling state next door.

After entering the seventeen digit alpha-numeric passcode for the VPN, for a slight nanosecond, The Hacker relished in the brilliance of his murderous plan. He had convinced himself long ago that he was on a divine mission. Denying his psychopathy, like all murderers, he was an optimist. He thoroughly believed the scriptural passage that said, *"To whom much was given, much would be expected."* He had been given much and now it was time to return the favor.

~

Anika was the living proof that wealth certainly had its privileges. As was her ritual, she disrobed to take full advantage of her in-home, wellness center's amenities. The steam room was her sanctuary.

She looked forward to topping off her fitness regime with the deep breathing exercises she had mastered as part of her yoga routine.

With her pole-dancing name of Sencerity, Anika really didn't need to maintain her profession. After all, she had accumulated plenty of money.

She reasoned, "'Why kill the golden goose,' as the Americans say."

Dancing was how she made her fortune and that was how she was going to continue to grow her burgeoning empire. She owed a lot of her "entertainment" success to Pilates and hot yoga, specifically Bikram-Yoga. The stretching, balance and strength poses helped take her exotic pole-dancing moves to an intensely higher level.

She was the envy of the club...the object of insatiable fantasies of both men and women.

It was a one-way fantasy.

To her it was all business and she would have it no other way. A car here, diamonds there, and there was always room for cash; and now this fabulous pad – her crowning achievement. She was truly amazed and disgusted by how stupid men and oftentimes women were. They would do anything for sex but not just for sex, but merely the prospect of sex. The more they believed that the fantasy mirrored reality, the more they were willing to part with their sanity and so much more. It was precisely because of this universal human weakness, she was able to professionally weaponize sex.

They got what they wanted and she got what she wanted. Fair trade.

She truly felt there was no one better than herself who could satisfy her needs. She even learned autoerotism, enabling her orgasms by mental acuity. Her relationships were as overrated as they were superfluous; a means to and end with the emphasis on the ends.

Senserity had no sympathy for fools.

As she eased her way into her custom made steam-room, one that could rival any found at the highest high-end private clubs, she found her spot, turned on the preset level of steam and laid back. She began taking in deeper and deeper breaths. She could feel herself reaching a higher metaphysical plane. As she concentrated on her breathing, all the remaining tension slipped from her body until she was totally oblivious – the state of Nirvana had taken over.

Accessing the electronic thermostatic gauge from the climate-controlled server room, The Hacker began to gradually increase the humidity level. The upsurge in hydrogen molecules created in the watertight room slowly absorbed the remaining oxygen, elevating carbon dioxide levels.

Sencerity's body was already completely limp from the alternating cycles of tension and relaxation from her workout. As her bronchial passageways continued to dilate, her breathing became more labored as her lungs filled with moisture. Although she could feel the heaviness of her breathing in her semiconscious state, no alarm bells went off tripping the fight or flight mechanism of her sympathetic nervous system.

Her unique ability to forestall panic was not due to genetic superiority or conversely a physical flaw but by right-of-passages earned in isolated sweat lodges in the remote wilderness of Sedona, Arizona. This was where Senserity set herself apart. The conditioning she acquired in Sedona rendered all other challenges painless. Where others failed, she succeeded in breaking through the highest level of physical, mental and spiritual limitations.

Her toned muscular system was rendered immobile as the decrease in lactic acid removed the stress from her body. Her completely relaxed state belied the true source of this peaceful seduction into darkness.

As she slipped into eternal bliss, The Hacker closed the electronic loop, confident that her death would be assumed as a freak accident. His many years of experience in these matters helped him visualize the eventual autopsy report stating the cause of death as acute respiratory acidosis due to alveolar hypo-ventilation.

Manner of death: accident.

Her passing would be as exotic as her life.

19

There were no latecomers to the second online session. Given the level of participation during the first gathering, Niles sensed rightly that enthusiasm might be high for this follow-up meeting but he did not expect that everyone would have signed-on fifteen minutes before schedule.

He and Tiffany were elated!

After briefly recounting significant high-points from session one and some feedback from the online questionnaires, Tiffany was ready to present the next topic for discussion. They both knew this could be explosive but it had to be done.

Tiffany/Jock asked, "In our last session we thoroughly discussed the role that our adversarial legal system has played in creating a hostile environment to resolve disputes of the heart. In your mind what respon-

sibilities does the so called winning party have in respect to the loser?"

"If you are asking what I think you are, the
winner better watch their back because, as they say,
'payback can be a mother...'" said Amazon.

"Amazon is right. It's all 3G," said Sheep.

"What do you mean by 3G? What the heck does
technology have to do with this?" queried Hockey Player.

"No, I'm talking about glee, greed and green.
I've been in and out of courtrooms enough to know that
winners don't care about the consequences of ill-gotten
gain. They believe that because they've won, winning
in itself is confirmation that they were right. The pleasure they take in hurting someone is almost greater
than the anticipation of getting their hands on someone's money. That sure was the case with my ex," said
Sheep.

"Yeah, that's the kind of stuff that makes you
want to hurt somebody," said Rock Star.

"Real talk," chimed Avenging Angel. "I mean it
is ridiculous what they get away with and then strut
around with their chests puffed out, bragging about how
they got one over on you."

"What bothers me the most," began Super Model, "is how when after you've been raped and pillaged
and publicly humiliated, there is no one that comes to
your aid. The lawyers are paid and gone; the judge has
quickly moved on to other cases, suffering no remorse
or fear of retribution for their lopsided decisions. There
are very few avenues for appeal. You've experienced a
kind of death but there are no grief counselors. It's like

a town without pity. The only thing you are left with is rage!"

"Yes," said Sheep, "and that blinding rage needs an outlet and I can't think of any target better than the jerks who caused it."

"That's all well and good," said Avenging Angel, "but I wonder at what point will a taker sincerely realize that even though they may have won, the prize is not worth the price of winning? Would it only be, at a literal knife point...a razor's edge between life and death? And would that realization remain with them once the threat was removed?"

"The proverbial moment of truth; that moment when we are all on the same page," stated Amazon.

"Like deathbed repentance." Chimed in Hockey Player.

"Stated differently," added Sheep, "is the question you are asking: 'If they could choose between legally stealing from someone and remaining alive, would they concede victory or would the pleasure they received from hurting someone be worth a literal life's sentence?'"

"Exactly! Would they trade their life for the victory?" asked Rock Star.

Just because you can, doesn't mean you should," Super Model said softly.

The heated debate continued.

But, it was clear to both scientists, the participants felt that the perpetrators did not fully comprehend the depth of the hurt and pain they inflicted, and if they did, they either didn't care or were lulled into the false sense of security that the law was on their side. And worse still, was that they trusted their opponents, would remain law-abiding citizens and thus present no threat for their absolute victories.

It became evident to the researchers that there was more than a need to recapture monetary losses. It appeared that money was just the scorecard, not the game.

The real loss was that of faith...faith that if one did right – right would be done in return. Once faith was destroyed and once one's belief system was shattered, it could very well be the tipping point where even the most normal person could be transformed into a vengeful blood-lustful beast. In the absence of faith, one differs little from man's lower-brow cousins. The ensuing vacuum of rationality could subsequently be filled by the de-evolutionary desire for survival: kill or be killed.

Winning could prove to be deadly.

The participants' remarks became increasingly aggressive.

Absent throughout the exchanges were any contribution from Court Jester.

Niles decided to try and subtly get him to add his perspective. "Last time, Court Jester, you had an interesting twist on our discussion as it related to the lengths we would go to preserve our freedom. Any thoughts on the matter now at hand?" asked Basketball Referee.

The Court Jester, with his hands folded in front of him and his legs propped up on the banister answered, "No, not really."

"I'm surprised. Last time you seemed to hold a sort of insider's perspective. I'm curious as to what may have influenced or changed your point of view?" Asked The Ref.

"I never said that my point of view had changed. Actually it hasn't. The only change is my situation." The Court Jester said casually.

"How so, if you don't mind sharing?" The Ref pressed.

"My adversary is no longer." Continued The Court Jester.

"No longer what? No longer your adversary?" The Ref asked trying to understand.

"That too, but no longer as in 'dead.'" Said The Court Jester in an emphatic tone.

The collective gasps and sighs of the group resembled the sound of a bottle when uncorked for a second time.

"That is a change. How does that make you feel?" asked Referee.

With all eyes focused on him, Court Jester rocked himself in his chair, then said, "Just fine."

"Dude, you should be feeling a lot better than that! If it were me, I would be celebrating my butt off! How did she die?" laughed Hockey Player.

"I don't have all the details but let's just say it looks like she may have choked on her own greed."

The comments were rapidly blurted out:

"Dang!"

"Snap!"

"Wow!"

"I wish I were you!"

"Me too!"

"Hate to say it but I second that!"

It was difficult to identify their origins.

"On that note, I think this is as good a moment as any to end this session." Concluded the Ref.

Reality rushed in on all the participants, the animated high of the conversation clearly released pent-up endorphins. The rush was tempered by the sobriety of death.

All the participants reflected on their own personal values and pondered whether or not they could actually live up to their own rhetoric. It was one thing to talk about eliminating your adversary but another thing entirely in actually doing it or have it done, as the case may be.

Unspoken but unquestionably, each participant harbored a little envy and more critically, wondered if Court Jester perpetrated his ex's demise.

It was just too convenient. Too coincidental. Too unbelievably wonderful!

20

As soon as it ended Niles and Tiffany resumed the work they were doing, before the session began.

Tiffany turned to him and said: "He did it."

"You don't know that."

"Technically you're right but he sure seems guilty to me."

"Why is that?"

"My brother-in-law."

"What do you mean, your brother-in-law?"

"Court Jester had the same cavalier attitude that my brother-in-law had after he killed my sister and then tried to hide it."

"Tiffany, I didn't realize that, that had happened to you."

"It's not something you go around talking about. A murder in the family makes people feel uncomfortable, as if you have a contagious disease. They feel compelled to say they're sorry and look as if they pity you. And I surely don't need anyone's pity!"

"With all respect to your brother-in-law, that's not proof that the Jester did it. In fact, it's not really our concern and I don't think it's wise to pass judgment in absence of facts."

"Circumstantial."

"Tiffany, I'm beginning to worry about you lately," said Niles. "You're blurting out one word comments that make no sense. Are you okay?"

"Circumstantial evidence."

"Two words is not a huge improvement."

"Fine. What I mean is, most crimes are solved on the basis of circumstantial evidence, right? You have to admit that Court Jester has a strong motive. All you have to do is look at the file you put together on him and it's clear that, that he's wanted...no? He needed to get rid of her. In fact, he had far more to gain by killing his ex, out of all the participants. His situation was the most embarrassing and if his case were to go public, he would lose the most."

"You may be right about the motive but putting on my lawyer's hat for a minute, you only have one out of the three deadly ingredients to make a lethal soup. You still need means and opportunity."

"Two."

"You're regressing."

"Sorry, but I have an idea of a possible means. Check this article from the *Dessert Sun* on the Internet. Apparently she died at home - his home or more correctly his former home that he stupidly gave to her.
"It says that she was a very healthy twenty-nine-year-old with no chronic problems. It gives a lot of detail

about her background as a dancer, her multiple broken engagements with resulting restraining orders from men that claimed she conned them out of expensive possessions.

"Also, the documents regarding the transfer of ownership of the house have been sealed by the courts. No doubt a requirement by Court Jester's lawyers. The article goes on to state many other facts in the case but nowhere does it say that she choked to death."

"Am I missing something?" asked Niles. "I do not see how that proves means."

"Don't you remember what the Jester said? 'She choked on her own greed.' How would he know that? It's the same thing that happened to my former brother-in-law. He knew information only the killer would have known and that's how he got caught."

"Interesting, but how do you know that she choked?"

"I don't, but her body was found in her steam room. If we find out she choked, then we have a problem."

"What do you mean, 'we have a problem?' We didn't killer her."

"That's true but we may be sitting on information that the police could use in their investigation and I'm not sure but isn't that a crime?"

"Sure, obstruction of justice and withholding information in most circumstances is a crime but in this situation it is not discoverable by a court of law because therapy sessions are protected by the doctor-client privilege."

"Yes, but that's our problem. Remember, what we are doing here is not classified as a therapy. We are criminal scientists doing research, not offering psycho-analysis."

"Touché. The student has become the teacher."

~

  While Zeke was giving Sumi a detailed update on the progress that Slave Driver was making with ADEP, her mind kept wandering back to the last online session.

  "Just like that, and Court Jester's problems were over! Could it possibly be that simple? He must have done it or had someone do it for him. But where does one go to get someone who specializes in that line of work?" She pondered, 'What am I thinking? Snap out of it! I can't just have Brad killed!'

  "Sumi? Sumi!" Zeke called out.

  "Huh, what?"

  "Where were you? I'm quite happy to talk to myself, but since you're here, we might as well have a two-way conversation."

  "Sorry, I blanked out for a minute. It must be fatigue."

  "Did you hear anything I said?"

  "Sure. Continue."

  "You could at least do a better job lying about it."

  "Stop whining and just make me catch up."

  "I was saying that Slave Driver had no problem making the connections and consolidating the necessary power. There were a few glitches in the digital breaking and entering but he got through all the firewalls. We may need to adjust the launch time parameters a bit but

ADEP is working fine and surprisingly faster than my original expectations. We are a little more than halfway through the process with about 627 out of 1080 lines of pixels at last count.

"What I can tell you is that since I can see a little cleavage, it must be a woman! Actually, the fact that the image is missing an Adam's apple is a dead giveaway. Whoever this subject is, I know one thing...she is gorgeous!"

"How do you know that?"

"Because unless things have gone completely wrong, it appears as if she possesses the Divine Ratio."

"The what?"

"You know, the Divine Ratio...the perfect ratio or the beauty ratio of 1:1.677."

"I still don't know what you're talking about."

"It's the universal relationship between objects that denote ultimate symmetry. It's the reason why people like Brad Pitt and Hallie Berry are considered universally beautiful. It's the perfect relationship between the position of nose to mouth, mouth to chin and distance between the eyes, etc. Whoever this woman is, she is going to be beautiful!"

No one had ever told Sumi that she was beautiful. It was her sister to whom all the attention went to. Sumi considered herself less than average. But the truth was that although Rebe was quite attractive, she had to work at it. Sumi, on the other hand, was a natural beauty who did everything she could to downplay and hide it – the way she dressed, the plain manner she did her hair, her poor choice in the selection and application of makeup – all this underscored the profound insecurities she held onto since childhood days.

And while all along she was learning English, a new language for her, and also, meanwhile all the American kids were making fun of her Asian eyes.

Kids could be cruel but in this case, they were dead wrong. Sumi was a knockout by any measure but her negative internal voice kept this truth suppressed. Instead of trading on her looks as some had done – even perfected; Sumi let her brilliant mind light up her path.

What she was confronted with from Zeke, left her speechless. By not having a point of reference, she was now being hit with new and disaffirming information. Despite the magnificence of her mind and scientific objectivity, Sumi was struggling to adjust.

"The good news is that when we'll meet again this week," said Zeke, "most, or all of the process will be completed and we will know how viable the program is when we compare it to the actual test case."

"Okay," said Sumi, wanting to run out of there, "I will see you Thursday."

Sumi debated whether she should tell Zeke now or wait. And let him be surprised when he'd recognize that she, was – in the beta test.

She reasoned that their science would be better served if Zeke eventually came to it on his own without any prompting.

21

Jurisdiction had always been a problem when it came to law enforcement. If it wasn't the city cops fighting with the sheriff, it was the sheriff or state police squabbling with the FBI. Even though this case crossed over multiple state lines, plainly within the domain of the FBI, Nolen Roussard, even in his role as FBI – SAC knew he needed the cooperation of the local authorities.

For Roussard, this new murder, which he had been recently assigned, had the potential of being a career-making case.

His résumé was already punctuated with the apprehension of all types of killers that used unusual methods in their craft.

One of the cleverest murders he and his team ever tracked down, was that of a killer who had used an Ariel Drone to snuff out a lone golfer at a country club.

Nolen had even worked on cases involving serial killers, product tampering, slave trafficking, and fugitive captures; but this one was the most intriguing yet for him.

He often marveled at the imagination and innovation of killers. The professional or career murderers were the hardest to catch usually due to the absence of a direct connection to the victim but most of them eventually slipped up. A good cop knows that he can afford to make many mistakes but a killer only has to make one.

But this newly assigned case was surely going to test the limits of the Bureau's capabilities.

Nolen had to admit, even though luck was on their side, the Las Vegas Metropolitan Police Department did a fine job in its preliminary investigation. He knew that luck was just another advantage chip that had to be exploited with deft skills; otherwise it would be squandered.

As a policy, the LVMPD investigated each death with an eye to rule out homicide, as opposed to assuming that even the most obvious of deaths were accidental...or from natural causes. That was one reason why, they enjoyed one of the highest homicidal clear-rates in the country.

To the coroner the victim had suffocated due to fluid buildup in the lungs...ostensibly, by drowning. However, a veteran crime scene investigator noticed that there was a huge disconnect between the body temperature and the manual dial on the thermostat in the steam room. Luck was at play. This discrepancy had been duly noted in his police report.

Sensing a possible product liability lawsuit, and the victim's physical state, they appointed an estate attorney, who had the heating system checked out for malfunctions by a HVAC (heating ventilation and air conditioning), specialist. To the attorney's dismay, the specialist stated that there were no defects in the installation or detectable product failures, and suggested that because it was a so-called "smart home," suggested to the attorney that he should also consult with the vendor and installer of the electronic master control-system.

When the representative of the electronics company, who installed the server, preformed a diagnostic systems-check, from the print-out, all the recent data entries – revealed the master server had been accessed from the outside.

By itself, this was not an unusual occurrence since that was the purpose of the VPN (Virtual Private Network) application; but what caught his attention was the time that the camera in the wellness center panned, then froze on the steam room. This was the exact same time, which the electronic temperature override for the thermostat had been turned way up to maximum. It meant that while the victim had set the desired level as shown by the manual dial, the setting had been overridden by a command from the server from an outside source.

The representative said, "If an owner is at home using the steam room, why would he or she control the server using the Internet when they could easily do it from the internal Intranet?"

This meant murder.

The LVMPD realizing they did not have the resources to track all the dynamic IP addresses found on the server's log – reluctantly called in the Fibbies.

The case was assigned to Nolen's department because they had the best computer forensics team in the Tri-State area.

In Nolen's many years of experience, he had never imagined that a house could be used as a murder weapon. This was a first. It made him wonder if the Internet was a blessing or a curse...perhaps both.

The killer had been very adept at covering his tracks. He used multiple proxy servers and dummy IP switching sites all around the world, which were used primarily to identity thieves specializing in credit card and bank fraud.

As a result of 9/11, all the worldwide Internet traffic has been flowing through a nondescript building in the Bay area of California where every byte, thanks to the Patriot Act, has been cloned by the NSA through a switching node maintained by AT&T.

Given the quantity and quality of the gargantuan mountains of extraneous information, the key has been to decipher what to look for.

With the assistance of the FBI's computer technicians and cyber security analysts at Quantico, Nolen's team was granted permission to use a proprietary non-commercially available reverse IP locator. After a few weeks they were able to unmask the cloaking channels used by the killer.

Although Nolen had to be patient and let the techies do their investigative work, he wasn't surprised when they were successful in finding the source server. What he was not ready for, was, where the server was located. They traced the break-in of the VPN to the Downtown Los County Angeles Law Library.

The DT-LAW was one of the most prestigious law libraries in the nation. Given California's penchant for tort litigation, it was also one of the busiest. There were hundreds of thousands of visitors who'd use it each year. And just about every major law firm in the country had a satellite office in Los Angeles. It was stocked with most, if not all, of Black's Law Books. DT-LAW's catalogues were incredibly vast, they were rivaled only by the Library of Congress.

Nolen was baffled.

'A law library used as a crime scene to break the law? To commit a murder?' he wondered, 'This should be one for the *Harvard Law Review*!'

On the first floor of the library most lawyers and law clerks preformed research or used the computers to access international law libraries around the world for real-time legal decisions – mostly affecting commerce.

Additionally, there was a section along the north -facing wall, which had about sixty computer terminals where one could type briefs and prepare cases. One of the benefits to working in the library was that with so many lawyers present, it was a convenient place to get second opinions on thorny or arcane legal issues.

Not all the computers in the library were alike. Most of them were used for typing, so they did not typically have a ten-key keypad. Since many lawyers took up law because they were mathematically challen-ged, they had little use for the four computers, which were configured with the ten-key keyboard.

When Nolen found the one, which was one of those seldom-used computers as the source terminal, he

instinctively made the connection that whoever ope-
rated it was familiar and comfortable with the use of
numbers.

It caused quite a stir when the agents marched in
to cordon off and removed the machines.

———

At the crime lab, the forensic scientists went
through their routine task of dismantling the computers,
performing presumptive tests for blood, dusting for
fingerprints and cloning the hard drives. They checked
all the recent Google, Yahoo and Bing search histories.

Aside from the expected legal journals and porn
sites that a lot of lawyers visited and billed to their clients under the guise of professional research, there was
one CPU that had registered a hit on a members-only
password hacking site that used a cyber-security company as its front. Amazing how innovative criminals
were and how gullible consumers could be – a perverse,
yet arguably perfect match.

Nolen was confident that the forensic scientists
would come up with some useful leads, he also knew
that he would have to rely on some old-fashioned police
work.

All killers, including professional ones, usually
differed from case-to-case, but the principles for murder
remained the same. One-time amateur, serial or professional killers had in common was their obedience to
their MOM: Motive Opportunity and Means.

Contrary to popular opinion there was no such
thing as a senseless killing.

It always made sense to someone.

Nolen believed murder to be like algebra. If one had two of the three variables, someone more than likely, could solve the third part of the equation and hence find the killer. Nolen was fairly sure, he had both number two and number three.

The obvious number two was "the opportunity" made available via the Internet through the VPN gateway.

Number three, "the means," was the house itself and more specifically, the steam room.

The key would be the discovery of "the motive."

He was under no illusions; there was no need to reinvent the wheel. The motivation for murder, even a complex case such as this, was simple: money, sex, or revenge.

If the three failed to explain it, there was always the corollary of the first: more money.

22

"As I was saying," droned on the brilliant young cyber analyst, "We performed the diagnostic on the hard-drive. We were able to recall the data from the D-Ram and all the MMS and S-Ram chips."

"I don't mean to cut you off," said Nolen, "I am sure you followed all the right procedural steps and I am confident that your report will stand up in court but could you do me a favor and just get to the point? It's been more than two weeks since the murder and we need to keep things moving before the leads get cold."

"Sure, no problem," said the analyst. "Here is the short-hand version: Apparently the killer had a keen understating of the victim's routine, preset the control-temperature settings to go off a week later like writing a post-dated check. Although this is key evidence, even if we were able to trace his steps back to the Law Library, the video surveillance tapes would be of no help in identifying him because they are routinely written-over every seven days."

"What about DNA?" Anxiously asked Nolen.

"That's the good news. Whoever your suspect is, he is has some familiarity and comfort with math." Responded the analyst.

"How do you know that?" Nolen inquired.

"Easy, it's a well-known fact that most lawyers are mathematically challenged. That's why they are lawyers and not scientists or finance nerds."

"As much as agree with your professional dig, I don't get where you're going with this." Impatiently stated Nolen.

"Well, most people that work with computers use the keypads at the top of the board to input numbers. Not your boy. He used the ten-key numeric pad at the right side." Explained the analyst.

"I still don't get it." Said Nolen.

"Okay," continued the analyst. "Have you ever watched a person expertly use a ten-keypad, like a cashier at a grocery store or an accountant? It's very impressive how fast they are with their fingers flying all around without looking and making very few, if any, mistakes?"

"Yeah, I always feel intimidated when I see that," said Nolen.

"Don't be. They use a little-known secret. On the '#5' button, there is a little raised bump called 'the nipple key.' You will find it on non-digital telephone keypads, computer keyboards that have a separate ten-keypad, as well as cash registers and such. The nipple key is used as a position locater and as long as users keep their middle finger in that position, they will always know where their other digits are without having to look down with their eyes.

"But the reason why this is important to us, is that when he used the '#5' key, that little bump acted as a scraper and the epithelial stem cells containing DNA, rubbed off the tip of his finger!"

"And so?" inquired Nolen.

"And so, we were able to lift traces of DNA off the #5 key and run a profile. Unfortunately, it doesn't match anyone in CODIS at this time but nonetheless we now have our killer. We just don't know who he is or what he look like. At least not yet."

"Great work! I knew you lab-boys would come through! But one question: you keep referring to 'he.' How do you know it's a male?"

"When we did the DNA profile, we also looked for specific genetic markers that identify sex and ethnicity. The ancestral markers we found identified our suspect as a white male of most likely Middle Eastern or Jewish decent." Said the analyst.

"Great! That narrows our suspect pool down to about fifty million people." Nolen said throwing his pencil on his desk.

"Sorry, I wish I could tell you more but unfortunately we are limited to just basic info." Sighed the analyst.

"No problem, I think I know someone who could help us get past the limitations." Nolen half talking to himself.

The analyst quickly sitting straight up in his chair, asked, "Who?"

"Nothing. Have someone send over a usable sample of the DNA profile. You made my day!" Nolen said with a lilt in his voice.

"Always here to help."

Nolen didn't waste any time and called his sister -in-law Sumi Kim. Although he had to settle in leaving her a message to call him back, nothing could damper his enthusiasm.

His fervor was interrupted by a call from the case detective of the LVMPD. The question they all wondered aloud, was how could a stripper, even one with all the obvious talents of Senserity, afford to live as lavishly as she did.

The case detective methodically laid out all the details to Nolen.

"The victim, twenty-nine year old Anika Stradi-vinskya, professionally known as 'Senserity,' was a Russian immigrant with as a colorful background as her stage performance was titillating. Anika was a part-time student at UNLV, taking mostly graduate online classes majoring in Economic Psychology. She was an above-average student occasionally making the Dean's List.

"Apparently she was well-adept at capturing the property of well-heeled men as she was capturing their imagination. Although there was no record of her ever being married, she had a history of several wrecked engagements that led her poor-broken-hearted saps bleeding all the way to the banks.

"Over the past three years, Anika had amassed an impressive collection of "gifts" and other expensive items. Her bounty was not just random cars, jewelry or cash, unique to the spoils of her trade; apparently, when Anika pursued her prey, she went 'big game' hunting. She had accumulated a small fortune that included securities, homes, and other treasures, some of which were gained through civil settlements.

"Unfortunately, at the request of both parties, most of the case records were sealed by the presiding judge and therefore yielded no details."

This was no real surprise to Nolen.

The case detective continued, "Senserity's men, especially her most wealthy and accomplished men, would not want all their proclivities and frailties put out on public blast like scarlet letters of yore or more likely featured on the front covers of tell-all rag magazines.

"One thing that could be said for Anika's honorable character: 'she would always give back the engagement rings.'"

After listening intently to the detective's report, Nolen began to speculate as to whether he was dealing with a possible Russian mob hit or just plain old vanilla revenge. After all, some of the gentlemen's clubs in Las Vegas were run by some shady characters. That, along with wide spread speculations of Russian involvement in organized prostitution and human trafficking; it was not a big leap to expand their criminal enterprises to extortion.

'There was a good case for one of her marks; after losing his money and mind, his consequent craving to get his pound of flesh (or in this case 110 pounds of flesh) was amped up.' Nolen thought.

He knew it would be premature to lock on to any one theory or rule out any possibilities. One thing Nolen was certain of: given the unique circumstances of the murder, the killer was somehow familiar with the house and the house was worth a lot of money.

Following the investigative credo: "Follow the money," Nolen had no doubt that whatever road Senserity followed to get that house, would be the path that would lead back to her murderer.

Nolen's thoughts were consistent with what the FBI profiler at Quantico, Matt Garrick had concluded. Based on the crime scene and Anika' background, Matt suggested that the perp had a close association with the victim and although the murder was committed at a distance, it was nonetheless very personal to him.

Matt said, "The remote nature of the crime suggested that it was difficult or impossible for the killer to get up close to the personal space of the victim, such as in the case of a shooting or a knifepoint execution.

"Considering the fact that the murderer used the computer system of the home, indicated that he was intimately familiar with the inner workings of the house."

Matt recommended to Nolen; "Look closely at the previous owners who had either a personal or business relationship with the victim."

Although the court records were sealed, the gag order did not apply to title records. They remained public domain.

Nolen ordered a full title history of the house. Fortunately, there were only two previous owners.

During construction, the title was in the name of a Nevada LLC. Checking with the Nevada Department of Corporations, Nolen's team was able to ascertain that the LLC had one member: E. Thomas Wasserman III.

The background check on Wasserman revealed that he had a privileged pedigree. He was well-educated white male who came from a wealthy Jewish-American east coast family. Although he currently resided in Los

Angeles, Mr. Wasserman spent a great deal of his time in Las Vegas since he was an avid golfer – with single-digit handicap. He had built his home purposely on the most exclusive private golf course in southern Las Vegas.

Nolen's back hair stood up when he found that Wasserman was a practicing lawyer.

Nolen knew from his legal experience that if he focused solely on Wasserman, it could be a thorny issue at trial. Defense lawyers would claim that the police had never developed any other suspects or leads.

Nolen felt that Wasserman looked good for this crime, but realized that everything would come down to the DNA evidence. He was confident that with his sister -in-law Sumi's help he could remove all doubt.

He was determined to benefit from her knowledge to his advantage.

23

"It's you!" Zeke said, almost screaming into the phone.

"What do you mean?" Sumi answered but failed at trying to play dumb.

"Don't play with me, you know what I'm talking about." Zeke snapped

"Okay, what are you saying?" Sumi surrendered.

"I'm saying ADEP works to a 'T' and I am looking at a 3D image of a beautiful young lady of Asian descent who has a remarkable resemblance to Sumi Kim. That's what I'm saying!"

"Zeke, that's wonderful. I can't wait to see it!"

"By the way, I took the liberty to age progress the image to sixty and congratulations you'll still be marriage material! I can also tell you that you're going to age gracefully."

"Thanks, I'm not concerned about that." Sumi said.

"You might not be concerned but whoever you get married to, will have a vested interest in who he'll be waking up to, in thirty years."

"Men!" Sumi exclaimed.

"What?" Zeke said with mock surprise.

"You guys can be so shallow." She replied.

"Shallow, maybe, but stupid, not." Zeke said with conviction.

"Whatever." Sumi said nonchalantly.

"Look, as I've said, ADEP works perfectly but we still need to tweak the color contrast and refine some of the parameters. As you know, we are only able to manually control for such things as hair length and style. By the way, you really look good as a blonde."

"I'm not blonde." Sumi said a bit annoyed.

"I was just playing round with hair color. You should consider trying it." Zeke said glibly.

"Never!" Sumi shouted.

"Blonde Asian is hot!"

"You're incredible!"

"Can't wait till I work on the full-body module."

"I'm sure I know why." Sumi said exasperatingly.

"You bet!" Zeke said enthusiastically.

"I have to return a few calls and I have a 2:30 P.M. meeting here for about an hour. I can make it to your place around 5:00."

"I'll be waiting with the Champagne chilling on ice!" Zeke said with a tinge of glee.

"See you then." Sumi said as she hung up the phone.

Sumi was extremely excited and could hardly maintain her focus during the meeting. It occurred to her that even if the beta test had gone as well as Zeke had said, using herself as the prototype could backfire. What she needed was an independent subject, preferably one who'd demonstrate the broad application of the system.

Looking over her phone messages, her brother-in-law Nolen had left a message.

A thought came to mind.

~

"Sumi, thanks for returning my call."

"No problem, Nolen. How're my sister and the kids?"

"The usual...the kids are a handful and Rebe is on the war path but everyone's fine."

"Good, what's up?" Sumi asked.

"I have a situation – a case to be exact. I'm not sure how far along you are with that computer program you've been working on but I would truly appreciate any help you can give me."

"Your timing is impeccable! I just got word that our beta test was a success."

"Congratulations!" Nolen said sincerely.

"Thank you. Now tell me about your situation."

Nolen explained all the details of what the Bureau had dubbed as the "VPN" murderer.

"I have a suspect who looks good for the crime, but I'm going to need some corroborating evidence against him. The profiler gave an age range of thirty-five to fifty-five years old, white male."

"Don't tell me any other physical details of the suspect. This will maintain professional neutrality."

She made it clear that they would have to be very careful and document each step of the process beyond the requirements of criminal courts to satisfy the peer review scrutiny that would be sure to come. She outlined the protocols and the timeline and gave him a list of items she would need.

"Oh, Nolen, you and any of the agents or criminalists who'll be exposed to ADEP will have to sign the requisite confidentiality/non-disclosure agreements."

Nolen had already anticipated some of these requirements. "I'll have them delivered to you by tomorrow morning."

They shared a common surge of excitement as they discussed the possibilities of what this breakthrough could mean.

Out of curiosity Sumi asked, "The cause of death?"

Nolen humorously quipped, "Let's just say... she choked on her own greed."

Sumi was rattled for a moment.

'Where have I heard that?' She thought.

She tried to brush it off as a mere coincidence ...perhaps it was nothing more than a mild déjà vu.

24

E. Thomas Wasserman no stranger to the Federal Building in Westwood, a few blocks down the street from UCLA, was a bit nervous. Even though he had been there on behalf of his clients many times, what was nagging him this morning, was the timing.

The assistant to the DA wasn't helpful either; over the phone, he refused to give Tom the reason behind the vague request to meet with the SAC.

Lately for E. Thomas Wasserman, there had been a lot going on, both professionally and personally …and now this.

As he drove his black late-model Aston Martin through the unguarded entrance at the corner of Federal Way and Wilshire Boulevard, a random thought came to mind, 'That the facility, although serving as a very important symbol, is at the same time paradoxically vulnerable.' As this though coursed through the unregulated road of his mind, he became aware, 'That the appearance of freedom may be just as powerful a deterrent as the display of strength.'

His trepidation grew with each step he took up the staircase of the austere grey-white building.

'What is this all about?' he pondered.

In his mind, it could only be one of two things, and since Senserity's death was a local and not a federal issue, it could only be one. Nevertheless, Tom had to admit he was a little apprehensive and had to be careful on how to comport himself.

He knew the authorities would likely want to talk with him and that was why he informally rehearsed but for now he could not afford to come off too practiced.

Even before the interview, Nolen felt confident that he had the right guy. Call it a hunch, call it instinct or call it intuition honed by years of experience, it really didn't matter.

To Nolen, Wasserman had the means, the opportunity and the motive. The unholy trifecta!

Nolan's confidence was bolstered by the "insurance policy" he took out by having Sumi run her DNA model. When that was done, he would have his perp dead to rites. This initial chat he was about to have – then leak to the press – "person of interest" was just a "let me make you sweat," oft used as a police tactic.

Nolen had done his homework.

But this was clearly an ingeniously orchestrated hit and Wasserman's credentials told the story that Nolen was not going to be dealing with the over-the-counter generic suspect. No, a person as clever and intelligent as Wasserman would have to be accorded some measure of respect. But the depth of his intelligence only made the case more interesting and his strength, if baited correctly, could become Wasserman's greatest weakness.

Nolen had seen it all before and figured he would see it again. He couldn't wait!

A background check on Wasserman gave more weight toward a motive.

Nolen's team discovered that in addition to conceding a substantial amount of assets to the victim, Wasserman could not risk exposure or adverse press due to the promise of his upcoming promotion; otherwise his high-profile clients might bolt on him.

E. Thomas Wasserman didn't need the money – prestige was a much more precious commodity than treasure itself. He was already filthy rich. It was billable hours that led him to the Holy Grail in making partner in the law firm. Wasserman, coming from a family of overachievers, this was the minimal way to distinguish himself, within the bloodline of authentic blue bloods.

～

In preparation for the interview, Nolen settled on the strategy of taking the indirect tack by bringing up a few issues in another case, which involved one of E. Thomas Wasserman's prior clients. Nolen used this ruse to serve as a distraction and allow Mr. Wasserman to get comfortable before he got hit over the head by the sledgehammer of the Stradivinskya affair.

If things went as planned, there would be a faint but noticeable change in Tom's demeanor – cops call this a *tick*.

~

Tom walked into the entrance on the North Wing. He went through the security checkpoint and dumped the contents of his pockets in a plastic bowl on the table in front of the metal detector. In the past, he considered this process a hassle disguised as a show of force. He had never paid the security officers any special attention or they to him. But today, he could swear they were looking at him differently – more intently.

'Am I just being paranoid?' he thought, 'Or are they detecting a change in me like a bloodhound pointing its tail? Does guilt really have a scent?'

He chastised himself for this momentary weakness in confidence and knew he had to get a firm grip before he'd trip himself up.

The office décor – government grey if austerity had a color this would be it. The severe surroundings were not a fashion faux pas but implemented by design. The inescapable message that disturbed one's stylistic sensibilities was one of no-nonsense, no excess and no forgiveness.

Thomas wondered, 'Who was the audience for this highly orchestrated ambiance? The visitors or government employees? Was this assault on the senses designed to make the visitor uncomfortable and prone to slip up? Or perhaps an effort to make the employees angry and thus needing to vent their frustration out on those non-indentured servants?'

He heard a voice.

"Mr. Wasserman, I presume?" said the attractive but out of place assistant. The contrast of the drab surroundings and her natural beauty were incongruent and seemed to jostle him from his reveries.

"Yes, how did you know?"

"Let's just say we have been anticipating your arrival. Please have a seat; Mr. Roussard will be with you shortly."

Thomas's discomfort was mounting as he sat in the outer office. First the security officers and now this overly familiar assistant; he kept reminding himself that there was nothing to be concerned about.

'Had he not followed the well thought out plan to a "T"? Despite their resources, the Feds would fail to connect him directly.' He was confident of that.

If the outer office could be described as '60s efficiency, Roussard's office could only be considered '70s retro. The mix of the gunmetal desk, plastic chairs, and green shag carpet was nauseating. The surroundings made him think of what it must have been like in a Stasi headquarters in East Germany during the cold war.

'Regardless of our astronomical fiscal deficits, what would a few dollars more, to upgrade this dump, have on our collective national debt? Surely, they could do better than this,' Thomas thought.

"Mr. Roussard will see you now and good luck!" said the assistant with a sort of Giaconda smile, which to him seemed to be more like a sneer.

Reluctantly he stepped inside Nolen's office.

"Nolen Roussard. Glad you could make it."

"Sure."

"I would assume you're wondering what this is all about."

"It did cross my mind."

"Let's not suspend the suspense, shall we?"

"That works for me."

"It appears that your client, a certain Mr. Melvin Mandeville has recently showed up on a very interesting list. A list of tax evaders arriving from the Swiss government as part of their new...how do I put this? 'Transparency program.' You know the Swiss; they have really come around to this new way of thinking since 9/11. They not only have provided us with this list of very unpatriotic tax evaders but they also threw in the names of their trustees. You wouldn't happen to know who Mandeville's trustee is, would, you?"

"Listen, you can't pin that on me. My client does not need my permission or my consent to name the trustee on his accounts here, in Switzerland or for that matter anywhere else in the world."

"You're right and you're wrong."

"How so?"

"You are correct in that he does not need your consent to name you as trustee to secret Swiss bank accounts, even if the intent of the scheme was not necessarily to avoid taxes. But to hide assets from the court and his soon-to-be ex-wife? Now that's a crime! And there's a catch here, Mr. Wasserman, we have proof that not only did you know and consent but you did it because you don't really trust your client. And I don't blame you, he's a liar and a cheat. Nonetheless, this was a clever way to insure that you got paid and that is where you are in the wrong. I believe I can pin it on you and I plan to."

This exchange went on for almost forty-five minutes.

E. Thomas actually felt relieved that he had guessed correctly and thankful that this meeting was about his low-life but rich client Melvin Mandeville. Adding to his sense of comfort was that he felt, he was well prepared to defend himself. He knew the government's case was weak, because in legal terms, advice is distinguished from consent. Just because he provided strategic advice for asset protection, did not mean that he suggested that his client follow it.

As far as Thomas was concerned, Melvin was on his own on this one. He was not going down for this albeit well-paying thug.

"Is that all you got?"

"We think it's enough."

"Then let's agree to disagree on that point. If there is nothing else, I have other matters to attend to."

Confidently, E. Thomas rose and took one and a half steps toward the door.

Nolen, paying homage to his favorite TV cop, Colombo, said, "There's just one more thing, a small matter really. Do you happened know or more accurately, did you used to know a young woman named Anika Stradivinskya, previously known professionally as Senserity?"

Stunned and completely caught off guard, E. Thomas froze in mid-stride. His broad smile turned upside down, like a bad imitation of the famed mime Marcel Marceau, as Thomas' euphoria sank to dread.

~

For the next two and two thirds an hour, Nolen Socratic-esquely peppered his prey, E. Thomas

Wasserman III, with a slew of questions. Nolen was very careful at first not to directly accuse E. Thomas. He didn't want him to lawyer up.

Nolen was content to keep E. Thomas dangling and talking. In this, he had his prime suspect helping him solve the riddle of Ms. Stradivinskya's murder.

E. Thomas was left wondering what the State's theory was.

By three o'clock they were losing interest in the nuanced conversation.

They both got what they wanted.

Nolen planted the seed of culpability and E. Thomas suspected what he was up against.

Nolen's last salvo was directed straight to the cerebellum. "Let's cut the BS, Mr. Wasserman. You and I have something in common. Something that binds us together. In fact, you could say it's our destiny."

"What are you talking about, 'our destiny?' You and I don't have as much as ant turd in common!"

"Oh, but we do. I may not have your Ivy League pedigree and we don't share the same country club memberships and social connections but we bloody well sure have something in common."

"And what on earth would that be, Mr. Roussard?"

"We both know who the perp is."

"And how would I know that?"

"Because, Mr. Ehud Thomas Wasserman...one, two, and three, you did it."

Thomas was stunned!

He felt like he was spinning out of control like a first day apprentice in a Whirling Dervish dance troop. He had not expected for things moving in this direction.

Attempting to maintain his balance E. Thomas un-
steadily rose and lumbered toward the door.

He turned and with a steady voice, said, "Prove
it!"

"And prove it I will! I just want to know one
last thing."

"What?"

"How does it feel?"

"How does what feel?"

"How does it feel to be bent over a cocktail
table and get your salad tossed as you are being rear-
ended by a circus clown? Because you know what?
That was what Senserity was...just a performer."

"Screw you!"

"No, Ehud Thomas the third...not screw-a-me,
screw-a-you!" Nolen said it in his best Korean accent,
then he continued in his normal voice, "Here you are,
one of the top family law lawyers in the state, maybe
the nation. Everyone that wants to win and has the
money to pay for it comes to you. You make your living by demolishing your opponents and making a train
wreck out of the lives of their clients. And you, 'THE
MAN,' had his rear handed to him by a stripper!

"You've probably had to bail out your clients that have
fallen to the same game dozens of times and laughed at
them as you've clocked up enormous billable hours to
save the poor bastards. If word got out that you've been
turned out and stripped naked by an unworthy opponent, it would deal a devastating blow to your career.

"You might not make partner. And that would wreak
havoc on your reputation on the country club circuit not
to mention the distain you'd reap from the family back
home.

"But I don't think that was your real motive. No, it goes much deeper than that. After all, you're already rich. I believe it hit you to your core that someone could do that to you. The gall of her! It insulted your blueblood sensibilities. Right?"

Not getting any response from E. Thomas, he continued, "Your family history doesn't demand that you always win, but it does demand that you exact revenge. Yes, I did my homework on you and your clan. Because, you see, you're not in Philadelphia, this is Los Angeles, and we don't play that bull around here. You are going down. And there's no do-over!"

E. Thomas stood there without saying another word, then he gave Nolen a look of utter contempt.

That last comment was still ringing in Thomas' ears as he made his way out the building.

25

Experienced social scientist doing primary research know that the law of diminishing interest makes no particular exception to research projects. Holding a subject or group of subjects' interest in a project past its emotional apex or the moment of catharsis is rare. It's because the subjects' interest and the scientists' interest are often misaligned and/or mistimed.

For the scientist, research, it's the beginning of a long and arduous process who's trying to explain why a certain behavior or phenomenon occurs in society for the purpose of predicting outcomes. For a participant. it's driven by more immediate goals such as finding a solution to a personal crisis or situation; for one it's long-term for the other it's short-term.

Niles and Tiffany were astonished that there was zero attrition for the online project, given that the rewards were only psychic in nature. This was important for two reasons: first, it implied that the subject was considered highly-important to the participants although that could have been influenced marginally by the selection process; and second, it helped prove the efficacy of the online research model.

The goals of the last session were to measure whether there was consensus as to alternatives in order to diffuse homicidal rage. Specifically, did this process help? Was a gateway to catharsis opened? And the secondary goal was to elicit recommendations for improvements to the current system that would allow for a more equitable resolution to dissolutions.

Tiffany opened the final session by welcoming and thanking the participants for their consistent attendance and invaluable input. When she laid out the goals for the new session, the participants were all eager to contribute. At one point, she thought things were going to get out of control, as everyone wanted to talk at the same time.

She and Niles realized that the subject of improving the current system was a serious hot-button issue.

Most, but not all, intellectually agreed that murder should be avoided. The problem they mutually pointed out was that when one is in a hotly-contested divorce or settlement case, intellect has no seat at the table.

It's all about pain and hurt.

Although one side may enjoy a momentary victory, the real winners are the lawyers on either side. At the end of the trial it is impossible to distinguish from the lawyers' bank accounts who won or who lost. They get paid either way. They neither lose sleep nor do they suffer reoccurring nightmares of becoming self-appointed executioners. It almost seems as if the system was designed so they could never lose.

Vegas must blush with envy.

~

Avenging Angel was the first to suggest that dissolution issues should be taken out of the current legal system and that civilian arbitration be used instead.

Hockey Player agreed and added that no one should be able to disproportionately benefit at the expense of others.

Rock Star stated that mandatory counseling be made available before and after a case is resolved to include possible financial ramifications.

Amazon took this point further and added that psychological evaluations must be submitted as part of the case files.

Court Jester, who typically remained quite during the sessions, suggested that judges be given broader powers not just to apply the law but also to impose fairness and be able to take into consideration things such as fraud, deception, and previous history; essentially throw out the whole notion of "NO FAULT" divorce. Most of the time, there is one party that is actually at fault.

This elicited spontaneous applause from the group.

Court Jester went on to identify that the fault in the "NO FAULT" statute, while it attempts to reduce recriminations and therefore make the court system more efficient; those positive gains are offset by the emotional loss that comes from being cheated and further exacerbates in an already hostile environment.

It was now time for the Jock (Tiffany) to initiate a discussion around recommendations on improving the marriage process.

Super Model started off by suggesting that given the "seriousness of marriage," there should be a competency test no less rigorous than what is required for a dog license.

Everyone readily agreed.

Hockey Player said that marriage should be as hard to get into as it is to get out and that all parties should know beforehand what the rules are and how they will be applied.

Amazon brought up the idea that every couple should have to sign a mandatory prenuptial agreement or at least demonstrate knowledge of the state's statute prior to obtaining a license.

Playing devil's advocate, the Ref asked, "Would this advance knowledge have a negative impact on society in that people might choose not to marry?"

The response was an immediate and firm "NO!"

The group agreed that the real negative impacts were the results of contested divorces. Since our society has disconnected having children with the need to marry, there would be a net benefit because an informed citizenry produces better decision makers. Only time will tell whether or not "alternative" family structures are superior to the traditional nuclear family.

Super Model commented, "Perhaps we should take marriage out of the purview of the State altogether. This would take the jurisdiction from the Department of

Corporations and thereby take the financial incentives for gamesmanship out of the equation."

Her comment was based on the rising trend toward reversing the tide of economic and educational disparity between the sexes.

She added, "It would work like removing the biases inherit in Affirmative Action."

Rock Star brought up the point that no one should be on the hook for someone else's welfare for more than five years. "The way the current system is setup benefits the unproductive and/or uneducated spouse.

"For example, if you were married for twenty years and were the sole bread winner, and for reasons beyond your control, it was determined that it would be best for you to divorce, you could be required to pay spousal support for an additional ten years whether you had children or not. And that this is in addition to splitting the accumulated assets.

"It's a perverse form of social welfare that is inherently unfair and truly un-American."

When the group began to repeat some of their earlier comments with very slight variations, Niles knew it was time to draw things to a conclusion. As he was giving instructions to the group about filling out the post project questionnaires, offhandedly, Hockey Player asked Court Jester, "How are things going since your problems are now over?"

Court Jester replied, "You're wrong, HP, my real problems have just begun."

He went on to supply details of his case and inform the group that he was now the prime suspect in the murder of his former girlfriend and adversary.

Hockey Player asked, "Did you do it?"

Court Jester replied, "From my experience, I know that guilt or innocence is irrelevant and that the FBI claims they can prove that I did it. Besides, my career is now ruined because everything I've tried to keep quiet is now fodder for public consumption."

The collective gasp from the group was palpable.

This open exchange took everyone for a loop. They were now witnesses to things they had only dreamt about. Here, they had before them, one of their own that took matters into his own hands and now he was going to reap the satisfaction and relief that came from taking responsibility for committing the ultimate sin but in Court Jester's case, the imperfect crime.

An unspoken question loomed in the cyber air like a lead balloon: "Was giving into your subconscious id worth it?"

No longer was it just wishful thinking or unbridled anger released into the ether protected by the cloak of their avatars.

This was now potently real.

The idea of the group continuing to periodically get together on Duexover.com outside of the presence of Scientists was suggested by the Hockey Player.

All the other participants immediately agreed and the name "The Changers" was chosen to identify the group.

～

Sumi knew that Court Jester was the suspect in the case she was working on with Nolen but she still could not comprehend the magnitude of this coincidence. It was unbelievable in its randomness. Sumi being connected directly to the murder suspect motivated her even more than her original desire for scientific breakthroughs or any certification by law enforcement.

This had now become personal.

She had bonded with the Deuxoverlife.com group and experienced her own catharsis in a way she had not previously imagined possible. She had received far more from her participation than she gave.

She was conflicted.

She had no idea whether her research was going to help convict or exonerate Court Jester. On one level she completely understood what Court Jester had been going through and was not mad at him for feeling the way he did. She too, like all the others in the group, had felt and had to deal with vengeful desires as she worked through her own settlement issues. But now she was ironically assisting the opposing side that would prosecute her, if she, like Court Jester, gave into the compelling but deadly desire for executing her own personal justice.

She shook off these thoughts and focused her attention on the urgent matters at hand.

Sumi called Zeke to get an updated on ADEP's progress.

26

Niles and Tiffany were both stunned and elated.

As they were having their own private wrap party inclusive of imbibing a glass of champagne, they could not believe how their theories were working themselves out in real time.

They were satisfied that they had obtained all the necessary data, not only to get published by a major journal such as *Scientific America*, but also to complete Tiffany's doctoral dissertation.

They were impressed with their accomplishment; especially the online component, which perceived their potential game changer in academic research. But they were also pleased with the quality of input that the group contributed.

The group made, among other things, seven powerful suggestions:

1.   Mandatory counseling before and after a marriage or divorce.

2.   Psychological evaluation at time of dissolution.

3.   Mandatory prenuptial agreements as standard operating procedures or proof of understating of state statutes prior to granting license to marry.

4.   Take marriage out of the Department of Corporations.

5.   In lieu of lawyer participation, employ arbitration to reconcile disputes.

6.   Remove social welfare component by limiting maximum support to five years and suspension of support if winning party fails to engage in immediate full time education or employment.

7.   Modify the "No Fault" statues and add contributing factors that consider financial accountability that places stricter time limits of support.

Niles and Tiffany discussed and agreed that a copy of the paper should be released to the State Legislature, topic for discussion due to several recent high-profile celebrity divorce cases.

Understanding that change comes to the legal process at glacial speed, the team was undaunted in their commitment to document and distribute their findings.

∼

Nolen had developed a close collegial relationship with Sebastian Cromwell, the Los Angeles County D.A..

Originally from Argentina, Sebastian, received a lot of fame for being the first Latino D.A. in the predominately Hispanic Los Angeles County. This fact always brought a smile to Nolen since "Seby" was only half Latino, the other half being Irish.

Celebrity always brings claim of ownership.

By bringing Seby in early to work on the case, proved to be a boon to nail E. Thomas Wasserman.

When cops present mostly circumstantial murder evidence, the D.A.'s job is to try and poke holes in it to make sure it won't wilt under the sunshine of a jury trial.

A prosecutor usually has only one shot at a murder conviction and with only a few bullets in the chamber, he or she is typically gun-shy about hastily bringing any case, let alone a high-profile one, to trial.

Seby knew that in the age of televised trials, careers are made or broken by the media.

'Where is Marsha Clark?' he reflected rhetorically.

This was the reason why he would not greenlight the arrest of E. Thomas; until he had iron-clad proof.

Even though, Nolen and Seby may have disagreed on the timing, they were on the same page about nailing the fair-haired prick.

Nolen didn't leak to Seby that he had a trump card, he couldn't wait to use.

True to his way of working, he had already prepared the arrest warrant.

~

Nolen had already begun to make all the necessary arrangements to bring his prey into his waiting net.

When Sumi called him that ADEP was just about done and gave him Zeke's address; Nolen was ablaze with excitement.

~

By the time he arrived at Zeke's abode, Nolen was on a mission. He didn't give a damn about where Zeke lived, nor did he care or pay attention to the décor.

Nolen moved about as if he owned the place. He greeted his sister-in-law perfunctorily. Nolen had not intended on being rude, he was just focused and in "go mode." He had a fish on the hook, and now was the time to reel him in!

Upon entering the boiler room, Nolen abruptly asked, "Okay, where is it?"

Zeke instantly fired up Slave Driver and the monitor morphed from grayish background to green screen. Slowly the pixilated lines of the holographic 3D image began to take shape.

Nolen's mouth was agape and his facial expression was marked with both fear and astonishment.

"Wait, this is wrong, it's all wrong!" said Nolen, visibly agitated.

"What do you mean?" questioned Sumi with a hint of offence.

"I mean Sumi, with all due respect and gratitude, your program doesn't work!"

"How can you say that?"

"This is not the guy, this is not our perp!"

"Look Nolen, I realize that ADEP is new, and we can make adjustments to some optional characteristics such as hair color and length. Or perhaps adjust for presumed age, but I assure you ADEP is based on sound science." Zeke defended both ADEP and Sumi.

"You can make all the adjustments in the world but that won't change the fact that this is not our man."

"How do you know?" asked Sumi.

"Because..." Nolen opened his briefcase and from a manila folder containing several photographs, retrieved a 5x7 color picture of Ehud Thomas Wasserman. Nolen continued, "This is our man, right here, and not in a million years would he ever evolve to look like this other guy you've come up with. Oh snap, this is not good! Ugh this was to be my final piece!"

"What's the problem?" Sumi inquired, completely puzzled.

"I don't expect you to understand but I have substantial proof that I have the right guy and a team of agents in front of his office waiting for my signal to arrest him. This is real bad."

"Well just call them off until this is all cleared up. We can check our calibrations and parameters to validate the results. I'm really sorry about this; we were confident that ADEP was ready." Sumi said with a sense of urgency in her voice.

"It's not that simple. I also leaked the arrest to the media and they're also setting up to capture and broadcast the Perp Walk. I had to do this quid pro quo as a professional courtesy."

"I see, but that's a different issue altogether, than whether or not ADEP got it right. Is it possible that you have the wrong person and maybe Court Jester is not the murderer after all?"

"Who in the hell is Court Jester?" blurted out Nolen.

"Oh sorry, I meant to say Mr. Wasserman." Sumi corrected herself.

Nolen looked at Niles and then at Sumi, confused.

"Nolen, we have built in multiple redundancies into ADEP and while it is possible that one system may fail, it is highly unlikely that all will go awry at the same time. We used the DNA sample you provided and ran the profile for a minimum of three times and then compared all three of them." Explained Zeke.

"I guess it's not impossible that we keyed in on the wrong suspect but he really looked good for this hit. He was the only one we developed who had all three necessary elements of motive, means, and opportunity. I would be shocked if he's not the one. Even if ADEP is right, I still have a lot of work to do and the first will be dealing with the media." Said Nolen disappointedly.

A dejected Nolen left the two scientists in the bowels of Zeke's bottom floor loft. But before leaving, he requested a copy of the DNA profile and several iterations of aged progressed photos of the digital image from ADEP's output. This could be one more chip he could cash in, to help solve this ever-expanding mystery.

～

Dealing with the media hounds was always a little above being bitten in the crotch by an army of fire ants and Nolen's hope was that his gaffe would not become public fodder.

"Thank God," he said aloud, as he went over how he had carefully nurtured and cultivated his media relationships. Calling them friendships was an overstatement. "Relationships" was a far better description, it denoted they both needed each other like parasites and mammals rely on each other to balance out their ecosystems.

This mess was the least of his problems; he still had a killer to catch.

After several excruciatingly painful conversations with his media contacts, Nolen had to make a few rather embarrassing admissions of jumping the gun. He offered them some promises of future scoops, with this, he was able to keep the hounds at bay.

He knew in order to maintain this tenuous credibility, he would have to make an irrefutable arrest.

And soon.

Max Deveraux

27

The government's agency, Department of Homeland Security (DHS) and its predecessors have been surreptitiously accumulating and consolidating image data from multiple sources. Most citizens in the USA get recorded almost one hundred times each day. They receive this information from Google tags, social networking sites, DMV's, prisons, police records, airport security, stoplights, police patrol scanners, customs, store cameras and many more sources.

These huge databases are used to identify individuals based on facial recognition software, which employ mathematical equations to identify relational points on human features. Since no two human faces, including identical twins, are exactly alike, they have proven to be reliable sources to confirm someone's identity.

Initially, this technology was developed for the Las Vegas casino industry as a means to identify card counters and other cheaters. Now it is used extensively by law enforcement all over the world to spot outlaws of every classification including terrorists, drug smugglers, international fugitives, as well as rowdy soccer fans known as hooligans.

Nolen, still felt confident that he had his man but now he had to first identify and clear this other inconvenient and unexpected new suspect before he moved in to bag Wasserman. Otherwise, the defense would rightfully claim shoddy police work and prosecutorial bias.

Armed with the several age-progressed images he had received from Sumi, Nolen called and sent copies to his colleagues at Quantico. He knew that with the new and unprecedented subpoena powers granted by way of the Patriot Act. DHS was under certain circumstances able to compel just about anyone to give them identity info on any suspect.

Such entities included: Facebook, Instagram, Linkedin, Google and other social media outlets, with the requisite pushback mostly for public relations purposes, given how they view personal privacy as a salable business asset.

Theory being, the DHS could run images against these huge databases of tagged pictures and possibly get a hit; and just in case Nolen was dealing with any revenge-minded Russian, he sent copies to his boys at Interpol, and lastly, to Wal-Mart for good measure.

~

"Sumi, I checked three times. He can say what he wants but ADEP did its job. I think your brother-in-law needs to be less narrow-minded. He was so ready to arrest the wrong dude!" Zeke said.

"Zeke, Nolen may be a bit over-confident and at times zealous but trust me, he's not a maverick. He's been doing his job for a long time and he's very good at it. I know that he is very ethical and honest and just like all of us, he is capable of making mistakes. And if a mistake has been made, he'll be the first to correct it."

"I'm just saying…"

"Okay, let's go over our protocols so we can document and validate our procedures. It's better that we catch our own errors, if any, rather than have some gung-ho, non-accomplished, want-to-make-a-name-for-himself hater do it for us." Sumi stated.

~

E. Thomas looked out from the tinted upper floor window of his Century City offices, he could not believe the sight he was seeing twenty-six stories below.

The entire street was abuzz with activity.

Every news outlet in town had a crew outside his building like buzzards circling their prey. Smelling a captive, it was like a roach-coach-convention with every kind of food and snack truck representing all the various ethnic cuisines germane to Los Angeles.

As soon as the first round of weak coffee got served and stale doughnuts got eaten, the crews started to break down their stations and packed things up. They were on their way to the next blood-letting, so they could be in time to uplink for the seven o'clock news!

Unbelievably, it didn't look as if Ehud Thomas Wasserman the Third was going to be crowned "Celebrity Arrest-Of-The-Day," at least not today.

~

The intensity of the meeting with agent Roussard, E. Thomas anticipated some type of sensational arrest. From that time on, he was preparing himself to turn this unwelcomed publicity to his advantage.

He chuckled, thinking about what they say in Hollywood, "'There is no such thing as bad publicity." One just has to know how to work it.' He reassured himself.

E. Thomas was a master at this game! He was formulating and visualizing how he was going to flip the script by claiming that all this was a grand conspiracy by fearful, unseen and shadowy people in high places targeting him because of his certain threat of torching opposing counsel to ashes.

He smiled at the thought with puffed-up pride.

He would pick the highest of profile cases!

He would be *THE* go-to guy! Forget becoming a mere partner; he would use this media storm to become his own national franchise.

His grandiose dreaming was becoming bigger than the tobacco and ambulance-chasing malpractice suits combined!

Yes, he was ready for it, but still wondered 'What the hell…!'

28

Interpol was first to report back.

They didn't have anything. The image yielded no hits. They were going to check further but weren't hopeful.

A few hours after the Interpol disappointment, Nolen got a call from Quantico. Expecting the same from the dark ops guys, Nolen was surprised, they had a lead on a possible hit but it didn't make any sense at all!

The agency's social media analyst asked him to proceed with extreme caution, since they could not substantiate their findings and due to the Non-Disclosure Agreement he signed with Sumi, did not allow him to disclose the original source of the comparison images. Thus the Office of Homeland Security could not validate the findings.

Even though they were forwarding their results to him anyway, this was under the condition that DHS's involvement was to remain anonymous. Given the heat they and the NSA had been receiving from Capitol Hill and in the press, they did not want to be associated with more controversy, especially if there was the slightest chance that they might be wrong.

Knowing how much the different agencies competed for credit, relevance, and budget, Nolen read this not so much as CIA protocol but CYA protocol! Good 'ole boys club at play!

Seeing right through this veneer, Nolen keenly understood that no self-respecting civil servant was going to stick their neck out and co-sign on what could potentially be a CLM (Career Limiting Move), no matter what his or her personal convictions were. Especially, not with a lifetime government pension including early retirement and full benefits at stake!

All along, Nolen felt this was just the familiar bureaucratic song and dance, but when he finally received the secure email transmission, he immediately understood the spook's trepidation.

~

What he saw on the twenty-four inch screen, was unbelievable!

Nolen had been wasting his time by putting aside Sumi's ADEP match and he never doubted that his investigation of E. Thomas Wasserman was going the wrong way.

This was surreal.

Nolen's trust in Sumi's technology was escalating fast. He could not argue that the images matched.

But the identity of this target was going to create a whole new set of problems.

Everything was so out of kilter, he knew he would be forced to start over.

~

A person of this stature, being a murder suspect, was beyond reality.

Nolen had to review the dossier at least three times before he could even consider accepting the report. He knew there had to be a reasonable explanation for the residual DNA and image findings.

'No way,' he thought. There was just no readily comprehensible explanation. 'Why would someone, so-well-respected as this guy, get himself involved in an unseemly murder case?'

It defied all reasonable logic.

He felt he was way over his head, on this one. He had to proceed with caution. He also knew that Seby would never move forward against this suspect without incontrovertible evidence.

Nolen was both sullen and dumfounded. He was getting tired and confused. He looked over once again the evidence he had to date: E. Thomas Wasserman had the means, opportunity, and motive. He fit the initial DNA findings of a white male of Jewish descent.

He had a match for the DNA captured from the crime scene and the ADEP's output. That was indisputable. But, what was the connection? What motive could this unusual suspect have?

Nolen had to acknowledge that this was going to be a tougher case than he had imagined.

But early on in his career, he had learned the value of objectivity, as to who the suspects would be along the road in the pursuit of truth. Law enforcement was not about personal preference but about the facts, wherever they might lead.

He now had to get some background on this Person-Of-Interest (POI.) This deep background could be done internally, underneath the radar without any threats of leaks.

He put the most trusted of his inner-circle on the case. Within a few days, Nolen was handed the findings.

The report back:

The target had engineered an outstanding career and reputation as being honorable and by the book. His personal life was uneventful. He was married with two college-aged children. He was an elected public official and had won four terms running unopposed each time, with the exception when an advocate for the homeless challenged him but to no avail. On the surface he was clean as '*Mr. Clean.*'

Looking a little deeper, Nolen found that "Mr. Clean" was an avid poker player occasionally visiting the Commerce Casino in the City of Commerce, but most of the time playing a regular Thursday night private game with his close friends.

As Nolen and the select members of his team went over the list of regular players, one team member recognized a judge whom he had worked with, while serving as a court officer.

To keep things low profile, Nolen had Tim Brown, the agent who had formerly worked for the judge, make the call to him at home. Nolen's thinking was; the Judge would be more relaxed there as opposed to his chambers and perhaps be more forth coming.

Tim made the call.

"Hi may I speak with Judge Perry?"

"Who's' calling?" a female voice answered, with what seemed to be a Swedish accent.

"An old friend."

"Does this old friend have a name?"

"Oh, sorry, I'm, Tim Brown"

"Ok, Mister Tim Brown please hold and I will see if Judge Perry will accept your call."

After a few minutes, which seemed more like an hour, Judge Perry answered.

"Hey Timmy, my boy, what a surprise, I didn't know you boys at the Fed had time to catch up with old fart's like me?"

"Well Judge I always consider you more of a mentor but that's not why I'm calling today".

"I see, is this official business?"

"Well sort of but I would still love to catch up with you another time."

"In that case let's dispense with the chit-chat and get to the point, shall we?"

"Sure Judge. I'm actually calling about your weekly poker game."

"Listen here Timmy, I can assure you there's nothing the Bureau could possibly be interested in."

The judge assured Tim that the game was low stakes and did not violate any gambling laws.

Tim assured the judge they were not interested in the game, just the players.

"I'm sure it is, but this is a delicate and highly confidential matter regarding background on one of your fellow players."

"Well, if you are familiar with our game, you must also know that most of the other players are my fellow colleagues on the bench, all except Morton of course, but he's there because every good table needs a sucker who is eager to part with his money," giggled the Judge.

"I'm sure that's true but actually I am calling about someone else"

Agent Brown stated the name of the suspect.

The Judge reacted, "What could you possibly want, with that card counting cheat? I'm just kidding of course he's as solid as they come. He's not been caught on tape with some little boys or anything like that, has he?"

"No."

"So what is it?"

Tim explained in details the reason for his call.

The Judge proved to be very helpful, even if at first, he struggled for a few moments about divulging any confidences. His reluctance was swept away by his desire to avoid getting tarnished with any type of scandal. It was just not worth it.

~

One seemingly innocuous connection coming from an occasional participant in the Thursday night rendezvous.

'Who would have thought?'

The Judge and Tim talked further, getting into the nitty gritty.

The Judge informed Tim that the POI seemed to be rather obsessed with the limitations on discretion that family law judges had when it came to character of the various sides in legal disputes. Judge Perry went on to say that the POI appeared to feel that the "no fault" clause hampered their ability to impose fairness in cases where one party was egregious in their actions or their lawyers were exceptionally clever in the exploitation and testing the limits of the statute.

During the games, the judges would all share the details of their various court cases. Sometimes it would result in laughter and at other times there would be a collective shaking of the heads. And at still others the exchanges would result in dead silence. These were moments when the POI was particularly emotionally distraught. Judge Perry and the others just passed it off as the occasional judicial fatigue.

~

Later Nolen checked the court records but could not find any direct connection with POI and the case of Stradivinskya vs. Wasserman.

He was perplexed.

Nolen and his team continued with the shadow background investigation. He found that one of the Thursday night players did have a case with the names of the respondent and the petitioners redacted, rare but typical in a sealed case. What piqued Nolen's interest was that it fit the time frame of the Stradivinskya vs. Wasserman case.

Every case has an arc to the story, which is so compelling that it seals the deal. An instantaneous neural connection, which hits the amygdale section of the brain and allows one to see the unobstructed pathway to truth. An "Ah ha!" moment. That moment hit Nolen like one thousand amps of light.

Nolen was informed, as he was doing the background check, that the POI was obsessed with numbers and did his undergraduate work in economics. Moreover, he spent as much time doing calculations for divorce settlements as he did listening to the various arguments of the respective counsels.

At times, some members of the court would see him looking up to his left as if accessing the prefrontal cortex or parietal lobe of the right hemisphere – the part of the brain responsible for number crunching. Despite the Disso-Master exhibits he would receive from the lawyers, this POI would rerun, the assets and liabilities and income statements himself, always insisting unlike other judges, on having a computer with a separate 10-keypad at his disposal.

And at that moment, Nolen knew!

After many hours conferring with Seby, with the requisite understanding that if all hell broke loose it would be Nolen and not Seby who would take the heat.

Nolen and his team got the green light and hatched what would become their most high-profile arrest in decades.

29

"I was so wrong," Nolen said sincerely into the phone.

"What do you mean?" Sumi questioned.

"I've learned that one's gut does not override the truth. I don't mean to talk in riddles but suffice it is to say that ADEP will change the world of law enforcement and you should be congratulated, if not celebrated!"

"Thanks, but I'm still confused." Said Sumi.

"I can't say much more for now, but just make sure you watch the five o'clock local news."

~

The arrest – top story on every local and national channel, blazing through the Internet at dizzying speed.

A dozen FBI agents led by Nolen Roussard stormed the Los Angeles Criminal Courts building on Figueroa Street sealing off anyone going in and preventing anyone going out. While the judge was presiding over a current trial, was arrested and shackled in his own courtroom. He appeared to make a move to reach for his personal weapon under his bench. However, two agents who were assigned to enter from his chamber overwhelmed both the judge and neutralized the bewildered bailiff.

The agents made the arrest without causing any causalities but nevertheless stunning the perplexed courtroom.

There were a few jurors and an audience member who needed minor medical attention but were immediately released with no major traumas being registered.

The arrest of Superior Court Judge Roland Pierce was sensational, at the very least. But the comments he made to the news media took everyone's breath away.

Instead to plead the customary, "I'm innocent," he confessed that he did murder Anika Stradivinskya.

But what caught everyone's attention was when Nolen, Seby and members of the LVMPD, standing on the steps in front of an impromptu podium replete with microphones, the soon to be former-judge-now-murder-suspect was asked "Why?" by a reporter.

In front of a gauntlet of cameras, he allowed himself to momentarily pause, then slightly looked up to his left to face the camera, he said, "I just righted a wrong that our out-of-control system would not let me do in the courtroom."

This reverberated throughout the world faster than the speed of a DJT-tweet.

~

For many weeks, Nolen pondered about this murder. Was it really over and done with?

It was not exactly clear to Nolen as to what motivated Judge Pierce to take the law literally in his own hands or to put a finer point on it: his fingertips. Perhaps it was hubris, maybe legal fatigue or just a vanilla variety of a psychological breakdown.

Thanks to Sumi, DNA analysis has taken a quantum leap forward and forced the bad guys to step up their game. From case insiders, it's been revealed that Dr. Sumi Kim has had a few other inventions, which would for sure aid law enforcement.

After Dr. Niles and the newly PhD. Tiffany Lane published their controversial research, they were met with the expected hostilities from those who had a vested interest in things remaining the same – namely the Legal Industry Association and Representation Solicitors or LIARS for short.

An unexpected source of support, for a more un-biased process of dispute resolution, came from wo-man's rights advocates all over the nation. The research report indicated, along with their internal surveys, showed more and more women were seeing their finances pared down, during divorces at unprecedented levels and this seemed to be causing the sweet melodic chime of wedding bells to be drowned out by the angry blare of a forewarning alarm.

The larger question, like the blade of a guillotine over the heads of the ignorant, uniformed, and love blind, remained on Nolen's mind, whatever one's view of love, divorce or finances, one would agree that our worth should be tied to one's own nor to the wealth of others, even if and especially if one had to die to prove it.

~

"Arlie, where did you find this joint? I didn't know it was even here." Said Nolen.

"That's because you have lost your patrol car roots. You've been stuck in that ivory Federal Building tower too long! All the real cops know where the best gourmet bakeries are." I commented as me and Nolen walked in the diner.

"Gourmet? More like a dive! I mean look at that thing it's literally a hole in the wall!"

"Yeah, no extra charge for the ambience."

"Whatever. So, what's up?"

"I'm still high off that Judge making our girl Senserity feel the heat, and I wants some more! What-da-ya-got? And don't be trying to hold anything back and saving it for those anorexic former beautify queen TV talking head reporters."

"Why you're always putting them down? What do you have against them?"

"What put down? Just because I might not be camera ready, when it comes to breaking a story, they have nothing on me!"

"True, but that's because you-know-who, feeds you all these tantalizing leads." He said with a tinge of sarcasm.

"C'mon Nolen we both use each other. But I'm the one who smokes them out by diving headlong into the grime and doing the dirty work that you guys avoid, because I'm not bound by those self-imposed hypocritical ethical standards."

"What you call Hypocritical, the rest of humanity calls The Law!"

"Same difference."

"You really should get a hold on that Asperger thing. One day it might prevent you from pumping the breaks when you really should, and then you cross over to the other side – as in 'The Darkside.'"

"Yeah whatever. As you undoubtedly already know, my so called 'condition,' which I call 'relentlessness' has helped you get from my count...at least two promotions!

"Relentlessness? Some would call it 'antisocial disorder' with a heavy dose of 'insensitivity.'"

"Semantics. And look how far Senserity, oops my bad, I mean 'sensitivity' got Anika? Anyway, I just think it must be such a thrill to do what everyone else secretly only thinks about doing but are too scared to let it rip! I can't wait till my turn. Uh oh... Freudian slip."

"Arlie, if I didn't know you better, that would scare me. But the problem is, I really do know you better, and you really do scare me!"

"Nolen, Let's be real, everybody has a list. If you could at least punch-off one name on that list and get away with it... wouldn't you do it?

"Ahh...The List."

www.ingramcontent.com/pod-product-compliance
Lightning Source LLC
Chambersburg PA
CBHW070838030726
47504CB00005B/1144